SLATTERY'S GUN SAYS NO

Steven C. Lawrence

Slattery is a slow-talking drifter who ranges the West from Canada to the Mexican border. He likes to take life slow and easy, and he can't understand how trouble keeps following him around. Slattery doesn't pick fights, but doesn't run from one either. He's happy to let his gun do all the talking. Make Slattery lose his temper and, mister, you're as good as six feet underground . . .

SLATTERY'S GUN SAYS NO

Steven C. Lawrence

Curley Publishing, Inc.
South Yarmouth, Ma.

Library of Congress Cataloging-in-Publication Data

Lawrence, Steven C.
  Slattery's gun says no / Steven C. Lawrence.
    p. cm.
  1. Large type books. I. Title.
[PS3562.A916S57 1990]
813'.54—dc20
ISBN 0–7927–0149–6 (lg. print)   89–23340
ISBN 0–7927–0175–5 (pbk.: lg. print)   CIP

Published in Large Print by arrangement with Donald
MacCampbell, Inc. in the United States, Canada, the U.K.
and British Commonwealth.

Distributed in Great Britain, Ireland and the
Commonwealth by CHIVERS LIBRARY SERVICES
LIMITED, Bath BA1 3HB, England.

Printed in Great Britain

Chapter One

Tom Slattery stood up the moment he felt the train begin to slow. The man sitting beside him, a young heavily built Mexican, was about to get up. He sat back again when Slattery touched his shoulder.

"No, Augustín. Stay here," Slattery told him. "If it's anything, keep the door at this end shut." He'd bent his long body, looking past the woman on his left who'd leaned forward close to the window. She stared worriedly at the horseman outside, riding along even with the engine, one arm raised in a wave at the engineer and fireman while he shouted to them.

"What do you think it is?" she asked Slattery. She was in her mid-twenties, the lines of concern cut deep into her beautiful face. The way she pressed forward accentuated the bulge of her bosom which strained against her low cut dress.

Slattery didn't answer. The rider was alone as far as he could tell; at least alone on this side of the train. The man didn't have his gun drawn. He kept abreast of the engine, still waving and shouting while he angled his

1

mount in nearer to the cab. The horse ran hard, the small bomb-bursts of yellow dust kicked up by its hoofs almost lost in the long afternoon leg shadows stretching east.

Two, three of the other passengers were starting to stand in the aisle. "Hold your seats," Slattery told them. "Don't crowd up 'til the train stops."

"It might be a robbery," one of the men said. "I've got my wife . . ."

"This isn't a robbery," Slattery said. "Not this close to Rock Spring." He moved along the aisle toward the front of the coach. He was large and deep chested, in his middle thirties. The look of a tough and capable man was clear on his weather-burned, clean-shaven face while he peered through each window he passed. He'd flipped open the button of his black coat when he'd stood. The gesture was as automatic as his wishing he hadn't left his Winchester with his horse and gear on the rear flatcar. The fact he'd ruled out the chance of a robbery meant nothing. If it did mean trouble, he'd have little distance with his .44 Colt. Only his carbine would give him distance.

The train jerked, slowed more now as stinking thick black smoke swept past the windows. To open the door would let the smoke pour into the coach, making it

2

far worse for the one or two passengers who already choked and coughed from the cinder smell. The horse and rider beyond the smeared glass was pulling away from the engine. His back remained turned to the almost stopped train while he headed toward a gather of cattle a quarter mile off along the broad Texas flat.

The dark-suited man and the woman in the second seat looked up at Slattery. "We're stopping," the man said in an Eastern accent. "We weren't supposed to stop here." He was thin and white-haired, though he was no older than fifty. "Why should we have to stop here?"

Before Slattery could answer, the man's wife said, "It could be for any reason, William." She was as thin as her husband, but her narrow snub-nosed face showed no concern. Her eyes flicked to her daughter seated back-to the coach wall facing her parents. The girl was a pretty blonde, about twenty. She wore no make-up and was as demurely clothed as her mother in a black unruffled dress buttoned high at her throat. The girl took her stare from the butt of the revolver that jutted out of Slattery's waistband when her mother added, "I'm sure the conductor will let us know. Now that we've reached the town."

3

She'd pointed through the grimed window at a lone shanty, its boards warped and grey under the late afternoon sun. A crude corral and another shed, then the more solid houses of Rock Spring began to march past their view.

"Your wife is right," Slattery said to the man. "Could be we'll be here only long enough to take on a passenger. Or maybe water."

William Hughes simply nodded. He looked dutifully at his wife, who watched the coach door. Their daughter offered Slattery a quick, apologetic smile, but he turned away as the door opened.

A cloud of greyish, coal-smelling smoke billowed in with the black-suited conductor. Shutting the door, he spoke loudly so everyone could hear. "We have to stop here," he announced, raising his voice to carry over the outbreak of coughing. "The track has been torn up about ten miles ahead. We'll have to stop until it's repaired."

"How long'll that take?" a male voice questioned. "I have to be in Fort Worth by Wednesday."

More voices began to add queries. The conductor silenced them. "The Company hired a stage and has it waitin' for those who want to keep on going. You can get

4

aboard at the station. You'll be in Fort Worth tomorrow."

Mrs. Hughes said firmly, "How long will we be held up, Conductor? My family and I have traveled from Mexico City to Estancia by stagecoach. We have no intention of getting into another stagecoach."

The conductor was flustered at her tone. "Well . . . I'm not sure. That puncher just yelled we had to stop. He said the sheriff and a posse were out at the break. They'll help a repair crew, but the section will have to be sent out from San Angelo."

"The sheriff and a posse," William Hughes said. "Why a posse?"

"Well, they aren't sure what happened," the conductor began. "It could've been buffalo."

"Buffalo don't run this far from the Staked Plains," a passenger cut in. "The tracks are pulled up, it coulda been road agents lookin' to hit the train after we passed this town. That or Comanche."

The low grumble of talk which went on died with the man's final few words. "Indians!" a female voice repeated. "Oh, Gerald!"

The conductor scanned the watching, waiting faces. His lips parted to phrase an answer. Slattery said, "There's no chance of

5

Comanche, is there, conductor? This town's twenty-five or thirty miles south of the settlements." He glanced around at the other passengers, letting a smile soften the leathery hardness of his tanned face. "Whatever it was, the law is handling it. And there is a stagecoach for everyone to keep going."

"That's right," the conductor agreed. "There'll be a second stage if we need it. The Line's taken care of everythin'."

The train gave a sudden jolt as the engine ground to a halt. The rear walls of the buildings of the business district slid past the windows. The thick wooden timbers of the station platform came into view.

The conductor held the door knob, announced, "Just move your bags onto the platform. We'll have them put aboard the stage."

Slattery turned and started down the aisle while the conductor opened and hooked the door back. The Mexican who had ridden beside Slattery was on his feet helping the woman in the blue dress pull a heavy cardboard suitcase from between the seats. Slattery peered through the window one last time before he reached them. Five hundred yards north of the siding four cowhands worked at a makeshift corral tallying their gather. Nothing moved but the men and

6

cattle in the vacant length of prairie that stretched long and flat toward the gentle rise of the distant Llano Estacado. No puncher would work that carelessly if there was an Indian threat, Slattery knew. But he was just as certain a sheriff's posse wouldn't go out after stray buffalo ... He took his eyes from the glass, straightened when the Mexican spoke.

"I will get your horse, Señor Tom," Augustín Vierra said. "I will bring it to the stage-coach."

Slattery shook his head. "You take Miss Wells' valise out for her, Augustín. The brakeman'll unload my horse."

The Mexican lifted the suitcase and moved along the narrow aisle behind the other passengers. Slattery backed between two seats to allow Lottie Wells to walk ahead of him. She paused, watching him. "You're coming along with the stage, aren't you?"

"I will soon as I see to King." He nodded to her and, as she turned, he followed her out onto the platform.

A large Concord with OVERLAND 22 stenciled on its varnished door waited to the left of the tiny box-like station office. While the first of the train's passengers climbed into the coach, the stage driver was up on the box

7

loading and carefully arranging each valise and box the conductor and the station master passed to him. The Mexican had halted beside four town boys gathered near the door to watch. He heaved Lottie Wells' suitcase onto the box and stepped aside to allow the Hughes family to climb aboard.

Neither William Hughes nor his wife and daughter moved. The small thin man said something to the Mexican that Slattery couldn't hear. Augustín Vierra reached out and took Lottie's elbow to help her onto the step plate. Slattery glanced around at the rear of the train. The brakeman had already led King off the flatcar. He'd left the big black gelding in the sunlight beyond the wide shadow thrown by the squat buildings.

Slattery touched the closest boy on the shoulder. "You know how to water a horse, son?"

"Sure." He was about eleven, his freckled face smiling under his mass of red hair. "Anyone can water a horse."

Slattery dug into his coat pocket and drew out a quarter. "Give my horse a drink and bring him back here."

"Yuh. Sure," the boy answered, looking at the coin. "The only trough's at the spring." He watched Slattery nod. Accompanied by his three companions, he ran toward the black.

8

Lottie Wells leaned out the window of the coach, her eyes on Slattery. The station master, closing the door behind Augustín, stared at the deep cleft below the woman's low-cut bodice. He glanced quickly away and back at the Hughes family when Lottie covered the open V with her hand.

"You'll be coming right along," Lottie said to Slattery. Her eyes were troubled, switched for an instant to the boys who led the black gelding into town.

"I'll be in Brownwood before you," Slattery told her. And he added to the Mexican, "You get to the herd before me, tell Lute Canby I said you're working with him on the remuda."

"Sí, Señor Tom." Anything else the Mexican intended to say was cut off as the stage driver cracked his whip. The coach rolled ahead and began to turn into the side street that led into the town.

Lottie Wells' hand waved out the window. Grinning, Slattery lifted his left hand and returned the wave. Still grinning, he moved toward the platform steps. He stopped when he heard the station master say, "You goin' near the hotel, Mister. Would you give Mr. Hughes a hand with his things?"

"Be glad to," Slattery answered. William Hughes held two expensive brown leather

9

suitcases. His wife stood beside the last two. She had been staring along the street after the stagecoach, her mouth tightened into a thin line of disgust. "We'll send from the hotel for the bags, William," she said. "This man doesn't have to go out of his way."

The station master said quickly, "There's no man to come after them, ma'am. The Perani's are the only ones there, and they can't handle them. Mr. Slattery's goin' in anyway." He bent and lifted the heavier leather valise and held it out to Slattery. Standing straight, he was as tall as Slattery's six-two. He was a few years older, perhaps forty, but his skin was as hard and tanned from living so long under the harsh Texas sun.

Slattery had both suitcases now. He waited. The lines of distaste hadn't left the older woman's mouth. She motioned to her daughter. The girl turned with her mother and descended the stairs ahead of her father.

The station master stood for a few moments longer alone on the platform, until Slattery and the smaller man were halfway along First to Boulder Street. The August sun low over the western horizon flashed in a shimmering dazzle from metal on a rancher's buggy tied at the livery barn's hitchrail. The same sun reflected in a reddish-yellow glare from the windows on the left side of First. The station master fingered into his watch pocket and then studied the time on his Waltham. He didn't move until Slattery had turned the corner. Finally, returning the watch to its proper place, he headed into his office.

The station door was open inward just as he reached it. Two cowhands stood there. The long whiskered face of the one who gripped the knob stared angrily at the station master.

"What you tryin', Lutz?" he questioned. "Sendin' that puncher in with them? You realize . . ."

"I realize you shouldn't be seen," Paul Lutz snapped. He jerked the door from the man's hand, closed it fast. Quickly he stepped to the window and looked at the train. Only the fireman was in sight, and his back was to the office while he oiled the engine from a long-spouted can. Lutz swung around on the pair. "The main thing is that none of you are seen here with me. You know that, Paxton."

"The main thing is that we get hold of that girl," said Joe Paxton, muttering a curse. He wore battered Levi's and a faded blue shirt which were filthy in contrast to the station master's pressed pants and white shirt. The second major difference was the two holstered six-guns Paxton had thonged down to his thighs. His stubbled chin jerked at his

11

companion, a tall man with sharp eyes and a hard jaw. He was dressed in black, and he also wore two six-guns.

"We coulda had her 'fore they got off them steps," Al Fox agreed. "We wouldn't've had to go startin' any fire. We done enough work tearin' up that track."

"There won't be a fire. Not now," Lutz told them. He gazed through the window to make certain the fireman hadn't left the engine. "That man out there's name is Slattery."

"Slattery," Paxton repeated, and Lutz caught the careful look that passed between the two. Fox said, "You figure they hired him to cover them? That's a lot of money walkin' 'round out there."

"They didn't hire him for anything," Lutz said emphatically. "Slattery stopped here two weeks ago trying to hire punchers to make a trail drive for some outfit around San Saba. That cattle they're branding on the flat is making the drive with them."

"So?" said Paxton. "We heard 'bout the drive in Wichita. We know 'bout this Slattery."

Paul Lutz smiled. "A man as handy with a gun as Slattery has enemies. We need something that will keep people's attention long enough for you to get the girl. The broken rail's got rid of the sheriff and most of the town men. You turn Concho loose on Slattery, he'd put on a show that would draw every last person out of the hotel."

The look that passed between Paxton and Fox showed no doubt. "Conch's no match for a fast gun," Paxton said. "It'll have to be with his fists, or his knife."

"I don't care what he uses," Lutz said. "As long as he gives the rest of you the time you need." He peered out the window. The fireman was through with his work. He and the engineer stepped away from the cab and headed into the town.

Lutz left the window, spoke quietly, confidently. "Get Concho ready to jump Slattery. Just make sure people know trouble is starting. I'll have the hotel back door opened and horses waiting the minute I hear the noise break out."

Ugo Perani had stood in the doorway of the flat-roofed Sorento House since the boys had yelled into the lobby that train passengers were coming to the hotel. The hotel owner had thought he'd recognized the big black horse the boys led. Now he was sure. Watching the two women crossing the street in front of the men, his round face broke into a broad smile. He called across his

13

shoulder. "Maria, come quick! Slattery has come back!"

Ugo's smile held while the women approached the porch steps. He was completely bald, with an immense belly that bulged out from beneath his brown vest. A thick greyish mustache hid the lines of middle age around his mouth. He chuckled aloud as he stepped forward to take the suitcases from William Hughes.

"Welcome. Welcome to Sorento House," he said to the women. He edged aside to allow them to enter the lobby. "Thomas," he added in his best Italianate English, "you did not believe you would come again."

"I missed Maria's cooking," said Slattery. His smile shifted to the fiftyish, heavy-bosomed woman who waited in the lobby for Mrs. Hughes and her daughter to pass her.

"You wanted chicken," Maria Perani said eagerly. She made an expressive gesture, then a face at her husband. "You fix the rooms. I will cook. For all of you."

Slattery shook his head. "I won't have time to eat." He set the suitcases down alongside the women at the tiny registration desk. "Mr. and Mrs. Hughes and their daughter will stay. I have to . . ."

"You will not eat?" Maria questioned. She said something hastily to her husband in

Italian. Both of them, as round and fat as the Hughes couple were thin, appeared small beside Slattery's tall height. Ugo flung up his hands in mock despair, looking from his wife to Slattery. "You must eat. For my Maria! She would not let you go if you do not eat!"

William Hughes said, "We'll be having dinner, Mr. Slattery. You've helped us. We'd be happy to have you join us."

Maria took a deep breath, watched Slattery with hope and pleasure. Mrs. Hughes coughed to get her husband's attention. Ugo set his suitcases down and reached out to grip the ones Slattery had carried.

Slattery laughed. "Just for some broiled chicken, Maria," he said.

Maria headed for the kitchen doorway beyond the second floor staircase. Ugo said, "The livery will feed your horse. You come right back here." He hurried the suitcases toward the stairs. "Two rooms. I have two up here."

Slattery nodded to the women, saw that the daughter didn't turn with her mother. She stood staring at him, hands at her sides. "Patricia!" her mother said across her shoulder.

Slattery turned on his bootheel, heard Mrs. Hughes say to her husband, "You had to ask

15

him. A man like that, traveling with that saloon woman." William Hughes' answer was lost to Slattery when he passed the doorway onto the porch.

He knew very little about the Hughes family, except they had been touring Mexico and the train had been held up half a day in Estancia until they had come across the Rio Grande. The mother's attitude toward Lottie Wells had been obvious enough when she'd gotten aboard the coach. She'd kept her husband and daughter at the very front. Lottie had worked in a saloon, Slattery thought fleetingly, but it would do any woman good to really come to know her ... He forgot the Hughes family while he walked up Boulder, past the general store, the closed door of the jail opposite and two saloons which faced each other across the dusty width of the street. Fifty yards ahead the boys were busy watering King at the trough to the left of the spring from which the town received its name.

Two huge boulders sat in the middle of the roadway. The spring which bubbled between them had been dug out and topped by a circular Mexican stone wall. The single tall mosshung water oak and the cluster of cottonwoods, darkly shaded now as the sun set, had been made into a small

16

New England-type park that separated the business and residential sections. King lifted his head from the trough when he caught Slattery's footfall. He jerked his long neck up, sprinkling water from his mouth onto the boys.

"Hey! Hey!" the redhead shouted. He gripped the black's bridle tightly, glanced at Slattery. "He's 'bout watered, mister. Boy, he's a great horse."

"You want to take him to the livery and have him grained and rubbed?"

"Yuh! Sure!" The other boys echoed that.

Slattery fingered into his pocket. He handed the quarter he drew out to the redhead. "You can all split this." The boys grinned. "Remember, I want him rubbed good. Tell the hostler."

"I will. Yuh, we will." They led the gelding back along the middle of the roadway. The four friends crowded in close together in front of the horse.

Slattery followed them slowly. The last traces of sunset had faded. The hazy summer dusk settled down on the town in a soft bluish darkness. Lamps went on in the stores and on porches. Passing a cross street, Slattery could see north beyond the railroad to the shadows of cattle and cowhands near the pole corral. He would have time to ride

17

out and speak to them before he left. They had been among the ranchers he'd talked to when he'd passed through on his way to the Rio Bravo, and he might be able to answer any questions which had come up . . .

"Stop there! You kids stop!"

The boys leading King froze where they were. The command had bellowed from the Drovers Bar. A giant of a man whose chest and shoulders bulged his checkered cowhand's shirt half-ran off the saloon steps. He was not wearing a gunbelt. He swore at the boys, raised a huge hairy arm threateningly at them. "Where'd you get that horse? Where'd you get it!"

The redhead dropped the bridle, backed away fearfully with his friends.

"That man . . ." the boy began, pointing behind the big cowhand.

"What man?" The tremendous shoulders hunched as the giant swung around on Slattery. "What man?"

"It's my horse," Slattery told him. "Pick up the bridle, son. Take him."

"You take him nowhere," the giant snarled, going into an ape-like crouch, his fists doubled into thick clubs. "You stole that horse, mister! I'm damnwell gettin' my horse back!"

18

Chapter Two

Slattery side-stepped toward the gelding to place himself between the cowhand and the boys. "King is my horse," he repeated calmly. "I brought him in on the train with me."

"The hell you did!" the huge man roared. "That black was stolen from me, I tell you!" He'd halted three feet from Slattery, let his eyes shift to the walks and porches, at the people who'd come outside to learn what the yelling was about. "You got my horse!" His stare rested on the hotel porch, returned to Slattery.

A coldness ran up Slattery's spine. Tautness knotted the muscles of his stomach. The last thing he wanted was a quarrel or a fight. The boys were too close to them. The majority of those who'd left the buildings to watch were women and children and the older men of the town. Ugo Perani stood on a chair to reach the porch lamp while he lit the wick. The young Hughes woman was in the lobby doorway. She moved outside beside the hotel owner, spoke to him.

Slattery held out the gelding's bridle.

"Take him along, boys," he told them. "This is a mistake. I'll straighten it out."

"It's no mistake!" the giant growled. He shifted his stance, placed his immense weight on the toes of both thick-soled shoes. Yet he made no motion to attack. He was very much aware of his audience, was judging them for some reason.

Footsteps kicked the dirt behind Slattery. Ugo Perani reached his side.

"What you make trouble for?" the Italian asked. "The horse is Slattery's. He was here two, three weeks ago with this horse."

One big fist rubbed at the giant's wide whiskered jaw.

"I saw the horse then," Perani went on. "That woman on my porch can tell you the horse was with Mr. Slattery in Estancia today."

The fist undoubled while the man listened, but the hand still rubbed along his jaw.

"Go back on the porch," Slattery told the hotelman. And, to the boys, "Take the horse. I'll pick him up at the livery, myself."

The huge man stood awkwardly in the middle of the thickly shadowed roadway as Slattery walked toward the hotel with Ugo Perani. Slattery watched the fearful, tense faces, the excitement of the children pressed against their mothers. The curtains of the middle second-story hotel room were pulled aside while William Hughes and his wife looked down at him. Their daughter hadn't moved on the porch.

Slattery let the heavy-set hotelman start up ahead of him. He was on the bottom step when the huge man cursed again. The loud clomp of his shoes were the only sound in the darkening street.

"You, damn you!" the giant bellowed. "You wait! I wanna talk to you!"

Perani paused. Slattery said, "Keep going, Ugo. Watch Miss Hughes and Maria."

He swung around, hearing the hotelman say to his wife who'd come up to the doorway, "Inside, Maria. Take the girl in with you! Up to her room!"

The big cowhand closed in on Slattery, swearing obscenely.

"You hold it right there," Slattery told him. "You know that isn't your horse. That's all we have to talk about."

"They'd lie for you, mister. They did lie! I want that horse!" He crouched low, ape-like, coming ahead. His glance flicked to the lobby doorway, was surer when it dropped again to Slattery.

A voice on Slattery's left said, "He'll break his neck! Get Vreeland!"

21

"We can't! He took the posse out! You know!"

A still hush fell over the onlookers. Ugo Perani was backed flush against the hotel wall. Slattery edged to the right. Something had changed the giant. He'd dragged his baiting out long enough, would attack no matter what was said. A fight had to be kept away from the women in the lobby. "I won't eat, Ugo," said Slattery. "Next time. Tell Maria." He stepped into the street.

The huge man's big head bobbed up and down once in understanding and, half-wild with enjoyment, he lunged forward. He gripped Slattery's coatsleeve, began to jerk him around.

Slattery dodged to the left, hooked his right elbow violently into the middle of the wide-open stomach. The force of the blow doubled over the thick body.

"That's enough," said Slattery tightly. "You come to the livery. I'll show you my papers."

"I don't wanna see your papers," the man grunted. He'd shaken off the effects of the blow, continued ahead in a more careful crouch. "I want you!"

Realizing he couldn't stand toe-to-toe and slug it out with a bullish type of brawler, Slattery inched away. He had to end this

22

fast or the brute's mighty weight and power would wear him down. He paused suddenly and feinted to draw the man in.

The bait was taken. The giant surged forward, throwing his powerful right in a vicious roundhouse. Slattery slid under the blow, kept coming forward. The quick movement forced the cowhand to backstep, giving Slattery the advantage.

He crowded the huge man, smashed solid lefts and rights into the stomach. His third blow struck looser muscle, the fourth and fifth went deeper. The cowhand cursed in confused rage. He dropped one hand to cover his middle. The other arm swung out, reached to grasp and hold onto Slattery's shoulders.

Slattery jerked his body aside. Finding only air, the giant floundered ahead clumsily. Slattery's right rose up, opened as it dropped in a long, straight line, chopping like a hickory singletree against the bullish neck. Air gushed from the cowhand's mouth. He began to go down.

Frenzied, emotional chatter went up behind Slattery on the hotel porch. The voice was familiar, female, but he gave it no attention. The brute, on his knees now, pushed himself erect with his left arm. His right hand reached along that leg, jerked

23

the pants up to expose a long-bladed knife strapped to the shinbone.

He had the handle in his grip, was almost straight and firm on his feet when Slattery swung from the waist. The uppercut smashed solidly into the center of the broad chest. The knife went flying back into the darkness, hitting the roadway as its owner dropped. He lay there choking, fought to squeeze air into his deflated lungs. He tried to push upward, but after the hopeless attempt he sprawled flat again, gathering all his remaining strength to get his breath.

Confusion and talk circled them. Slattery turned to the louder voices above him. William Hughes and his wife were on the porch with Ugo Perani. The woman shouted above the protests of the hotelman. "Where is she? She was down here!"

"Inside. Inside with Maria." The heavy Italian pushed past those at the doorway, followed by the thin woman and her husband.

Slattery forgot the prostrate cowhand. He'd reached the top step when the shrill scream came from inside.

He was through the doorway, his coat unbuttoned, the tail drawn aside, his fingers on his Colt's butt. He let his hand drop, knowing even before he'd reached the small dining room that a gun wouldn't help.

24

William Hughes stood a foot within the kitchen, one arm around his wife's shoulders. Ugo Perani knelt in the middle of the floor over his wife's body.

Slattery saw the blood on the woman's dark hair, along her forehead. Maria didn't move while her husband touched her face and pleaded with her to wake up.

"Wet a cloth," Slattery ordered. "Cold water, Ugo."

"Maria . . . My Maria. She is dead." His round body shook.

"She isn't dead. Water, Ugo." Slattery was on his knees beside Maria, his fingers feeling for the wound. She'd been struck a scant inch above the right temple. He pressed the vein, cut off the flow of blood.

"Where is she!" Mrs. Hughes cried. "You said Patricia came in with your wife!"

Ugo had turned from the sink with a dripping wet dishcloth. Mrs. Hughes reached for him to stop him, but he shook her off and dropped down beside his wife.

Slattery wrung out the cloth, then folded it. Mrs. Hughes was bent over him, her words were shrill, demanding. "She had my daughter with her! Where is she? Where?"

"Stand back and let her breathe," Slattery ordered. He pressed the cloth along the still forehead, held it there.

25

"My daughter!" Mrs. Hughes cried.

"Stand back," Slattery said. "Keep quiet until we can find out." Under his hand Maria's head moved. She moaned.

"Easy. Easy." Slattery said softly to her.

Maria's eyelids fluttered and closed. Slattery wet her brow, held the cloth just above her eyes. "Lie still, Maria. Stay still. What happened?"

A low mumble came from her lips. Mrs. Hughes bent low again. "Tell us! Please, please tell us?"

Maria's eyes opened. She focused on her husband. "Some men . . ." The eyes closed, opened on Slattery. ". . . took her . . . kept me in here. They took her with them."

Chapter Three

"Men," Slattery said. "How many, Maria?" Tenderly he dabbed at the blood on her forehead. "How many were there?"

"Four," she whispered. "In the lobby when we came in." Her stare was hazy now, and her eyes closed.

"They took my daughter?" Mrs. Hughes

questioned. "Where? Did they say anything about money? How much did they say?"

"Please," Ugo Perani begged. "Let her alone. You see how she is." He touched the thin woman's arm, but she shook him off.

"She must tell me," said Mrs. Hughes to Slattery. "She's the only one who knows." Her nose and mouth lowered to Maria's ear. "Did they say anything about money? How much do they want?"

Maria's eyes opened, glassily. She tried to focus on the woman. William Hughes was doubled over beside his wife. "I don't care how much," he said. "I want her back. I want my daughter. How much? Please, did they say?"

Maria's mouth opened. Her lips phrased a "No," but the word wasn't audible. The onlookers pressing in from the dining room doorway noisily opened a path, and a lanky white-haired and bespectacled man of about sixty pushed by them into the kitchen.

"Move these people out of here," the man said. He set the black bag he held on the floor and took the wet dishcloth from Slattery's fingers.

"She will be all right?" Ugo Perani was pleading. "Doctor, she will be all right?"

Doctor Marsten's long slim fingers opened

27

Maria's eyelids, then closed them. "Move them out," he told Slattery. And when Mrs. Hughes said, "She has to tell me. She saw the men . . ." He cut her off with, "She won't talk, not for a while. She's had a bad concussion."

"But she has to."

"Get this woman out of here," the doctor snapped sharply at William Hughes. He gave no more attention to anyone but Maria.

Mrs. Hughes stood straight, backed away from the doctor, her expression a mixture of fear and worry while her husband took her arm. Straightening, Slattery studied the kitchen's rear door, hooked on the inside. The crowd, mostly women and older men and children, had already started to clear the dining room doorway. Slattery walked directly to the rear lobby door. Outside, the small yard was black dark and empty. Beyond the long thick shadow thrown by the building, the sand was greyish under the rising moon. He couldn't hear any noise, not even a trace of sound touched the flat.

"Some men are gettin' horses," a voice said from the hotel lobby. "Pete Dawson's goin' after the sheriff."

It was the tall station master from the railroad. He was coatless, had evidently run in from his office when he'd heard the

28

commotion break out. Either that or word of the fight had been passed all through the town, Slattery thought. The taking of the girl had been very well planned. The trouble out in the street had been more than enough to cover the men who had her. He walked into the lobby past the station master.

"You're comin', aren't you?" the station master asked.

"They're gone," Slattery said. "There's no way of telling which direction they took in the dark."

"We gotta try," an old whiskered town man offered. "Lutz has sent a kid after the punchers at the corral. We'll have enough men."

"We will have enough," Paul Lutz repeated. "You'll come too, Mr. Slattery? I'll have your horse brought up."

"I'll come," Slattery said across his shoulder. He could see the doctor hadn't yet moved Maria Perani. Ugo waited with Mr. and Mrs. Hughes, his round, mustached face drawn and terrified while he stared down at his wife. Slattery moved onto the porch, past women who spoke in low hushed voices. "I saw the fight start," one was telling those around her. "Everyone was watching that. We never thought of what could happen." She noticed Slattery, stared directly at him as though he'd done something wrong to listen.

The huge man he'd fought was nowhere in sight. People stood in groups of two or three or four, conversing, their faces barely distinguishable in the lamplight and brightening roadway. He stepped off the porch and crossed Boulder toward the Drovers Bar. Northeast beyond the rooftops, the curved edge of the moon topped the far horizon, giving more illumination to the prairie each second. Slattery walked directly to the bartender on the saloon porch. He was an angular, square-faced man in a tan collarless shirt and black vest and pants. He watched Slattery carefully.

"That man who was in the fight," Slattery said to him. "He came out of here. Did he go back in?"

Nodding, the bartender said, "He did, but he went out through the storeroom. He had a horse out there."

"You know him?"

"Never saw him. He was only in for one drink. He didn't even finish it 'fore he spotted that horse of yours."

"You don't know his name?"

The long square head moved from side to side. "I don't know no more about him than I do you, mister. That's a fact."

Slattery passed the porch and went into the alleyway between the saloon and the barber's shop. Behind him a horse's hoofs clomped up the street. Ahead, the flat was silent and brownish-grey, the cattle herded near the pole corral vague black shapes low along the ground.

Slattery drew his Colt, held it ready as he turned into the yard. Nothing was in view except the saloon's outhouse and storage shed. No sound anywhere out here. The moon rose full and white while he stood there. The darkness changed, the station building, the motionless railroad train and tracks and the cattle gradually outlined against the broad prairie, as silvery and shining as rocks emerging from black water. The stars took on a sharp brightness, clear flakes of light in the bluish night. From somewhere among the thick planks of the railroad station came the brittle chirp of a cricket. Slattery jammed his revolver down below his waistband while he swung around. He retraced his path into Boulder, calming the anger he'd felt since he'd first realized exactly how and why he'd been attacked and used right here in the middle of the street.

Joe Paxton jerked back on the reins of his grey stallion. "Keep goin', Fox," he said to the

31

horseman directly in front of him. Al Fox didn't question the order, simply rode on with the girl he'd held in his saddle since they'd left the hotel yard. She'd tried to get loose and yell when they'd grabbed her, but the arm-twisting Paxton had given her had taken that fight away. Paxton watched the double shadow move off for a few seconds, made certain she'd give Fox no trouble. He gestured at the two riders who'd pulled up alongside him. "Hear it? . . . one horse, I make it."

The three sat in silence, strained to catch the sound Paxton had heard. They'd headed due south from Rock Spring, had swung west only when they were positive no one followed. Paxton had his Spencer clear of its boot. He pumped it slowly. Baine and Allerby both aimed their six-guns. A coyote howled off to the north. Its rising drawn-out wail broke at the end in a shower of yelps and echoed eerily along the flat. Paxton swore to himself. He couldn't understand how anyone could follow. Concho had kept the whole town's attention on him and Slattery. There hadn't been time for men to get horses. Even if they had, they would be headed south.

"Only one horse," Baine muttered. His slim dark figure shifted in the saddle. "There he is." His gunhand pointed east.

"Hold it," Paxton said aloud. "It's Concho."

Horse and rider had emerged from the darker shaded section of the flat into the silvery shine. The huge man's forward-leaning, awkward position of sitting a saddle was unmistakable.

"Concho," Paxton called. "Here, Concho. Over here."

The big rider reined his mount to the left straight toward them. He broke into talk the moment he stopped.

"We better keep goin'," he began.

"What in hell you pullin'?" Paxton questioned. "You were to deliver the note and stay in town." Close to the giant, he could see the swollen jaw and dried blood around his mouth.

"I lost, Joe," Concho Grady said. "That Slattery'll lead . . ."

"He can do all the leadin' he wants. Did you throw the rock through the station window?" He saw the wide bruised head nod, did not give Grady a chance to continue. "You get back there. How in hell you figure we're goin' to know when to get her in unless we have you to come out?"

"Lutz can do that. Joe, that Slattery is no fool."

"He was fool enough to tangle with you.

33

You get in there. Soon as Hughes has the money come out to the soddy."

"Slattery'll ask questions."

"Let him. You were wrong about the horse, that's all. You stick to that, he can't do one thing. When we go in to collect, you'll stay at Gann's. You're afraid of Slattery, you won't . . ."

Concho Grady swore hotly. "I ain't afraid of no man, Paxton." He started to turn his horse. "I figured you should know. That's all. Don't you worry 'bout Slattery."

"I'm not, Concho. I figure what he did to you, you'll see to him."

The huge man left without an answer. Beside Joe Paxton, Baine let out a low chuckle. Paxton grinned at him and Allerby, but when he spoke there was no humor in his voice. "Baine, catch him and tell him to keep north of the town 'til he swings in. Allerby and I'll go south again and lead any posse off track. Then you keep headin' due north 'til you strike the crick. They are followin', they'll damnwell not know which way we went."

"You brought your coats. Good," Paul Lutz said to the men who were gathering in front of the Sorento House. "We could be out all night."

34

"We'd better start," William Hughes told the others. "We've lost enough time already." He looked in through the lobby doorway from where he sat on a horse that had been brought from the livery barn. Mrs. Hughes stood beside Ugo Perani, not saying a word to the fat hotel owner. When he'd seen his wife's fear-filled expression hadn't changed, Hughes added to Slattery, "What do you think? They've had a half hour's start. A half hour gives them a good lead on us."

Slattery didn't answer for a moment. He sat King rigidly, feeling the horse's mood. After the long train ride the black gelding was anxious to get started. He kept swinging his heels, his hoofs chopping, and Slattery let him pivot. Ten men were already gathered, fourteen now that the four cowhands who'd been tallying cattle at the corral appeared from a cross street. Most of the town women and children were present on the walks and porches. They were as stirred up as their men at the way the girl had been taken. Although it was clear a lot of them would have been glad if they could keep their own husbands or fathers out of this, none tried to stop them. The attitude of the riders, young and old, all carrying either a rifle or a six-gun, made this a grim business they wouldn't back out of. Slowly Slattery shook his head.

35

"I don't think we'll find much, Mr. Hughes," he said. "We won't be able to hold to the tracks in the dark."

"But they'll get away. We have to try."

"They'll have to get in touch with you. They want money, and they'll make sure you know where to contact them." Ugo Perani had gone onto the porch. He halted at the edge of the top step doubtfully. Slattery said to him, "Don't you come, Ugo. Maria'll need you when she wakes up."

"I should go. Every man should go."

"No, your wife needs you," one of the older men told him. He was past seventy, short and boney, and so round-shouldered he hunched over his saddle, causing his long silky white hair to hang almost to the horn. He glanced at Paul Lutz. "We head due south, I say. Right after them."

Slattery said, "Not south. They wouldn't start out in the direction they intend to take. They wouldn't go east because they know the sheriff's posse is off toward there. They're headed either west or north."

"The tracks start south," Paul Lutz offered. "The only thing we can do is follow them the best we can."

"We'd lose too much time," Slattery said. He heard the low grumble of disagreement which his words caused. His gaze swept the

36

men. "Half of us should follow the tracks. Half ride due west to north."

"That's the best idea," agreed Lutz. He spoke to the whitehaired old man, gestured at the six horsemen closest to him. "You'll lead this half, Mr. Osgood. The rest of us will ride with Slattery." Without waiting for an answer, the tall station agent swung his pinto mare west along the roadway.

Slattery rode abreast of Lutz. King, after so much standing and fidgeting, strained to gallop. Slattery held him in while they passed the stone spring and the line of small white-painted homes beyond the square. Ahead, the prairie stretched out silver white under the floodlight moon, shaded in areas where the land dipped. The only other sign of motion, beside the horses and riders, was the cattle herded around the corral. They would be out all night, Slattery knew. The tracks they'd leave could obliterate any real trail which might be picked up in the morning. He was thinking of this when the first cow bawled behind them. Instantly he stopped King. His face was tight and watchful in the darkness.

Lutz reined in fast, silenced the talk that began as the riders behind had to pull their mounts away to avoid crowding. William Hughes' horse banged its rump against Lutz's. "We can't waste any time," the thin man began. His words dropped when he heard the bawling and the noise of the cattle moving about.

"That doesn't sound right," Lutz said. "Somethin's botherin' them."

Slattery spoke to one of the cowhands. "Did you leave anyone with the herd?"

"No, we figured they'd stay together 'til daybreak. Be easy 'nuff to haze them back anyway."

Slattery reached down and pulled his Winchester from its boot. "The rest of you keep heading west," he said. "I'll . . ."

"I'll go along with you," Paul Lutz cut in. He raised the carbine he'd brought even with his shoulders.

"Both of us might make too much noise," Slattery said. He straightened in the stirrups, stepped to the ground. "Lead my horse with you."

He moved away from the riders, kept low to hug the land shadows. The horses' hoofs continued on westward. Two minutes later he could make out the closest cows, still bawling with the peculiar sound that told him they were restless and bothered by something. It could be a wolf or coyote hunting for meat . . . if it was a man, Slattery realized he might have a gun aimed at him right now. With the moon so bright, a man could bide his time. The near cows had moved off to either side of him, bawling even louder.

Impatience prickled Slattery, but judgment held him back. He crouched lower, sure it was a man, or men. An animal would have run by now. Slattery strained his eyes, squinted against the darker shadows, watched and listened.

He was fifteen yards from the pole corral when something alerted him, a low scuff of a boot on sand, a nicker of a horse that was instantly killed. He made his dash forward, slammed his body to the ground when he'd covered only twenty feet.

The blast of the shot racketed across the flat. The bullet ripped the dirt yards behind him, in the spot he'd just left. Then silence followed.

Cattle plodded all around him, terrified, stampeding by instinct away from the direction of the shot, their dark shapes charging past the corral. Slattery's hesitation lasted only the length of time it took to push onto his knees and continue his dash for the corral. Before the rifle pounded again at him he'd dodged one wild bawling steer, then a second. He dropped prone under the closest pole.

The second bullet whined inches above his head, whacked into one of the running cattle with the noise of a loud hand clap. The animal screamed and went down kicking.

Slattery had the gunman spotted from the flash of the barrel, yet he didn't dare fire. There could be more than one, and a blast from his Winchester would let them know exactly where he was.

He lay silently, waited, strained eyes and ears for any sound, any blur of motion that would tell him what he had to know.

Chapter Four

Behind him the cow still screamed. To Slattery it was a thick piercing bellow. There was no other sound close by, just the drum of horses' hoofs far out on the flat to the west.

Slattery edged clear of the corral fence and moved forward. He'd done this all wrong. He had no way to tell who'd shot at him, whether it was someone that was a part of the kidnapping, or rustlers after the cattle. He'd had a chance at a surprise attack, but he'd let it slide through his grasp like water in a dry hole. The gunman could have crawled away, maybe not. If there were more than one, they must have spread out.

40

A shadow moved beyond the side of the corral, a dark hazy shift of black against the silver of the flat. Another shadow waited to the left of the first, larger than the one which was clearly a man. Slattery raised the Winchester, balanced it on his palm. He separated the target from the corral poles and shot high.

The gunman's weapon blasted into the air, almost drowned out the shrill shocked yell the man gave. Slattery was moving as he'd squeezed the trigger, rolling to the left, once, twice to escape the expected hail of bullets.

No more shots came.

The echo of his carbine died. The running hoofbeats were a hundred yards to his left; more came from the prairie to the east of Rock Spring. Close to him two sounds broke the quiet, the dying grunts of the cow, the groaning and gasping of a wounded man.

Slattery's hands were clammy. He waited for someone to call to the wounded man, for a companion to try helping him. But nothing happened.

Slowly Slattery stood, ready to drop prone fast if he drew fire. As slowly he walked towards the monotone of the man's groans.

The man was sprawled on his side ten yards from where he'd left his horse. His rifle lay within his reach, but he only gasped

41

and mumbled incoherently, one hand pressed tightly to his chest.

Slattery walked wide around him, his Winchester aimed in case the man reached for the rifle. It was the huge cowhand he'd fought. Slattery stepped close to him and knocked the rifle beyond his reach.

"Get up," Slattery said. "Up slow."

Concho Grady cursed in a steady stream of obscenity at Slattery. He was aware that riders approached from both the west and the east toward the town. He rolled to the left, as though he meant to stand, but instead he reached for his rifle.

"I'll kill you!" he cried, gripping the stock. "Kill you!"

Slattery's leg shot out. His booted foot caught the man in the pit of the stomach. The rifle went skidding along the ground. Concho Grady crashed back, crouched in the dust. Slattery stood over him.

"That fight was to cover the ones who took the girl," Slattery said. The lead rider turned around the corner of the corral at a wide angle. Paul Lutz called words to Slattery but Slattery paid no attention to him. "Where did they take her?"

"You find them," Concho spat.

"It'll go easier on you if you tell."

Concho swore. He shifted his weight so he

rested on his good side, then began to sit up. Paul Lutz had reined in, was climbing out of the saddle. "That one of them, Slattery?" he asked.

"He is. Watch him." Slattery glanced past the corral at the other riders. "Circle out. There may be more with him."

Concho rolled fast to the right. His big arm reached out in the movement, pulled a knife from the boot top and brought it up to throw.

"You won't stop..." was all he said before Slattery's quick-pumped carbine blasted two holes that punctured his chest and ripped clear through the thick body. Concho flopped back and lay still.

Paul Lutz was beside Slattery, his rifle aimed. "He was so fast, he almost had you," he said. He turned toward the riders coming around the corral. "Reb, one of your cows was hit," he yelled. He looked as quickly east, went on in a loud yet hopeful tone. "That's the sheriff. We'll have plenty men now!"

Slattery momentarily studied the horses and riders that approached. He stared down at the dead man, said to Lutz, "I told you to watch him."

"What ... he was too fast. I'm not that fast."

Slattery's stare shifted to Lutz. The tall man's expression was lost to him in the

43

moonlight. The lead riders of the sheriff's posse were almost to them. Slattery left the dead man, walked to meet the sheriff. Lutz stayed beside him. The station agent hurried a bit so he'd reach Vreeland's horse first.

"We sent Ted Naill to get you, Dan," Lutz said before the lawman stopped. "He was supposed to tell you."

"He told us," Vreeland said. "He met us comin' back. I sent him after the men who went south followin' the tracks." He was obviously tired from being out all day, a small, slender man who appeared frail while he eased himself clear of the saddle. He was dressed in ordinary cowhand's sombrero and a blue work shirt and gray trousers tucked into shin boots. His gunbelt had a flap holster that hid all except the butt end of his Army-issue .45. He kept one hand on the pommel of his light McLellan, leaned there as though resting while he studied the dead man.

"Slattery had to kill him," Lutz told the sheriff. "He was goin' to use that knife."

Vreeland's small thin face lifted to Slattery. "You sure he was one of them?"

"He was. He faked a fight in the street to cover up the men who took the girl."

"With you? You were the one he fought?"

"I don't know why he picked me, Sheriff.

44

Unless I was there in the street at the right time."

Nodding, Vreeland simply kept studying Slattery, his lean greyish features impassive. William Hughes came up behind Lutz and Slattery. He halted close to Vreeland and a heavy-set deputy with a star on his cowhide vest who'd dismounted alongside the sheriff.

Hughes said, "Sheriff, I'm so glad you're back. With all these men, we're bound to find where they took my daughter. We found tracks about a mile due west of here."

"We're not goin' out after your daughter. Not now." Vreeland glanced around at the man who'd ridden with him. They were as tired and saddle worn as himself. He felt into his shirt pocket and took out a large black Mexican cigar. "I'm havin' a man call the other gang in. They ride around all night, there wouldn't be a readable track we could pick up come daybreak."

"Those kidnappers could harm her," Hughes said, his voice rising. "Men like that might . . ."

"Whatever they might do," Vreeland told him, "it won't happen 'til after you give them what they want." He struck a match with his fingernail, stared past the flame while he lit the cigar. "Did you notify them in Fort Worth about this, Paul?"

45

"No," the station agent answered. "I . . . everythin' happened so quick, I didn't think. We got the men together to go out."

"Then you better get on the telegraph seein' as your company's responsible. And ask for a Federal Marshal. I want one in on this."

"I will. I'll go right now." He moved to step past the posse, and William Hughes said, "I'll go with you. I want to send a message."

Lutz and Hughes vanished behind the men crowded around Vreeland. Vreeland said to Slattery, "You'll be stayin'. You'll be with us tomorrow."

"Yes."

Nodding, the small lawman turned to the heavy-set deputy. "You handle this one, Kennedy. The rest of you get some sleep. I want you all saddled up at daybreak." With that he led his stallion on the bridle toward town.

Slattery followed along with the posse members. The women and children of Rock Spring waited on the walks for their men. The moment they appeared members of families began calling to one another. Small boys and girls ran to meet their fathers. Slattery crossed the moonlit width of Boulder and tied King at the hotel hitchrail. Mrs. Hughes watched what went on from her room window. Ugo

46

Perani waited just inside his lobby, his round face no less worried and drawn than it had been earlier.

"You got one of them," he said when Slattery entered. "The big one who caused the fight. The talk says it was him."

Slattery asked, "How is Maria?"

"Bad. Very bad." The fat man bit his lower lip, looked worriedly in through the kitchen doorway. "The doctor is still with her." He shook his head as though he did not understand. "She does not wake. They hit her so hard, she only opens her eyes. But she does not wake."

"The doctor knows what to do, Ugo. He'll . . ."

"He will help her. I keep telling myself. I know he will." Yet the round head shook doubtfully, his mouth tight. "I will get you a room key."

Hurried footfalls and the rustle of a dress came from the staircase. Mrs. Hughes hadn't reached the lobby when her husband ran in from the porch. He waved the paper he held at his wife.

"This note was thrown into the telegraph office." He called to her and Slattery and Perani. "It was tied to a rock and thrown through the station window."

His wife took the paper and read it. Hughes

47

looked seriously at Slattery. "The man you killed must have gone to the station to throw the stone through the window."

Mrs. Hughes said, "One hundred thousand dollars. Left on the railroad platform in ten stacks of ten thousand each. Pay it, William."

"I've already sent a telegram to Chamberlain in New York. He'll wire the money to Fort Worth."

Slattery said, "Mr. Hughes, paying that money won't promise you'll get your daughter back."

"You be quiet, you," Mrs. Hughes snapped. "My girl would be here, she'd be right here if you hadn't had that fight out there. We're going to pay the money. We don't want a posse to hunt for her. We don't want to do anything except pay the money and get our daughter back." She glued her eyes to Slattery, her hand that held the paper shaking. "Tell him, William. Tell him!"

"That's what we want," her husband said. "I'll tell the sheriff. We'll tell him."

Mr. and Mrs. Hughes walked through the lobby and stepped onto the porch. Beyond the doorway, Sheriff Vreeland was visible in the center of the street, surrounded by the citizens of Rock Spring. The man he spoke to was the angular, square-faced bartender from the Drovers Bar. Vreeland noticed the couple

48

leave the Sorento House, and he walked to meet them.

Slattery said to Ugo Perani. "I'll take that room now."

The hotelman picked a key from the rack, then led the way upstairs. He inserted the key in Room 24, four doors from the landing.

"I will make supper for you," the hotelman said.

"Don't bother, Ugo. Stay down near Maria. If there's anything I can do."

"I know you will help. It will give me something to do. Please, Thomas. I will get a steak."

Perani retraced his steps along the short hallway. Slattery pushed open the door. He glanced back at the landing when he caught the sheriff's voice on the stairs below.

Vreeland appeared with his heavy-set deputy. The deputy held a twin-barreled shotgun. He halted at the top of the steps while the sheriff approached Slattery alone. He seemed so small and slender as he'd been near the corral. But there was no trace of frailness to his brisk stride. His tiny black eyes watched Slattery closely.

"That puncher you shot, Slattery?" the lawman asked. "You say you never saw him before?"

"That's right."

"Rube Whaleen says he was waitin' over to the Drovers most of the afternoon. He went out back before the train come in. The agent saw him from the station watchin' you passengers get off."

Slattery nodded, made no move to shift his eyes from the lawman's. "He was in on what happened, Sheriff. He'd naturally be watching. The way I see it, his job was to make enough ruckus to cover the men inside the hotel. He did a good job of it."

"Because you happened to have your horse in the street. I call that fast thinkin'. Danged fast thinkin'."

"Sheriff, I was asked to come to this hotel."

"I know. The man who asked you is backin' you on that. I reckon you didn't know anythin' 'bout Hughes owning a string of shoe factories back East?"

Slattery simply kept watching the lawman.

Slowly, Vreeland nodded. "Well, you can see what it looks like, both of you strangers. Maria Perani never saw any of the others before either." He raised one hand slightly, gestured past the open doorway. "You just stay in there 'til this thing's settled."

Slattery said, "I don't get a chance to prove anything? That's all there is to it?"

"Has to be," Vreeland told him. "Now Hughes has asked we hold off a posse, I'd say you had your chance." He shifted his boots to leave, but then added, "You had no choice 'cept to kill that man?"

Slattery let out a long slow sigh. The irritation that had been riding him blossomed into anger. "He had his knife in his hand, Sheriff. You saw it out there."

Again Vreeland nodded. "That's the way Lutz saw it. You feel lucky he did. Just the same, you don't try leavin' 'til after we have that girl." He turned and retraced his steps to the landing. There, he halted a few moments and spoke to his deputy.

Slattery stood in the open doorway until the sheriff went down the stairs. The deputy remained, leaning against the wall, his eyes on Slattery while he cradled the scattergun in his arms. Slattery closed the door, began to take off his coat. He'd been locked in here, rather than the jail, only because a town man had spoken for him. He thought over what the station agent had stated about the dead man being near the tracks when the train had arrived. He'd watched the town's backside and the platform all the time the engine was stopping. He hadn't seen any man.

Slattery thought about that while he took off his string tie and rolled up his sleeves. He poured water from the pitcher into the enameled basin on the dresser. Outside of

51

William Hughes, the one person who'd been with him almost constantly since he'd stepped off the train was the station agent. He wondered about that, about exactly what he did owe this man Paul Lutz.

Chapter Five

Paul Lutz said, "I still don't know. Slattery went to the hotel because he was carrying those suitcases. I didn't have any idea it could be more than that." He looked along the length of the mahogany counter of the Drovers Bar. Only men were present under the thick haze of tobacco smoke that rose past the crowns of their hats to the ceiling lamps. Most had been members of the sheriff's posse. They'd stood with bootheels hooked onto the brass rail, listening to the bartender tell his version of what had happened. One or two muttered a curse, their language free and rough and masculine away from their women and children. Yet the women and children of Rock Spring weren't forgotten by their husbands and fathers. The closeness of the kidnapping to their homes was a reality which angered them, and something they feared.

"No, I was there when he took the suitcases. It's hard to believe he was planning anythin'."

"They had it planned to the minute," the bartender said in a flat drawl. "That dead one didn't move from that window once they were in the hotel. He knew Slattery was headin' up to the spring. They had it planned all right."

A low growl of assent murmured along the bar. Paul Lutz studied the faces. He hadn't expected a development like this, but it was exactly what was needed. The one thing which might put him in danger of suspicion was the fact the money was to be left at the railroad station. With all the attention being given to Slattery, there was little chance of that.

"I'm just sayin' what I think." The station agent's tone was definite. "I know what could happen if Mrs. Perani dies. I've got to say what I believe."

"Had to be someone on the inside," a stocky, bow-legged puncher said. "You know how Slattery stopped here couple weeks back. Two days he spent here. He knew the town good as we do."

"What 'bout that trail drive?" another puncher questioned. He was taller and thinner than the man next to him, his long face just as tanned and leathery. "If he was

53

only setting things up, the whole idea could be a bluff."

"It ain't," a rancher said. "I've worked too long and hard on that gather of cows out there."

"Still, it could be," the bow-legged rider said. "We shoulda checked on him before we went out. He was lyin', he should be strung up just for that."

Divided conversation filled the room. The ranchers who'd gone ahead on Slattery's word that a major cattle drive would leave from the San Saba in late August wanted no part of the idea their work and hope was wasted. They depended too much on the promise of a beef market in the newly opened government range country in Wyoming, Montana and the Dakotas. The drive meant an endless market for their Longhorns. Now, with the whiskey making them heady and resentful, none wanted to even allow others to express opinions that everything was for nothing.

"The trail drive is real," Paul Lutz said. "I've received messages on the telegraph about it. That's what makes me wonder about Slattery."

"I don't wonder 'bout him," the bartender stated. "I know."

Sheriff Vreeland's entrance brought a heavy hush. The scrawny little lawman paused momentarily opposite the backbar mirror, then stepped into a space the drinkers hastily made for him. Rube Whaleen filled a jigger and set it in front of Vreeland. The sheriff emptied the shot with a toss of his head.

"You get anything out of him, Dan?" the bartender asked.

Dan Vreeland twirled the shot glass in his fingers. "He still claims they used him," he said. "He's stayin' in there 'til after it's settled." He looked at the bow-legged cowhand. "Marble's takin' the alley 'til ten, Cooper. You willin' to stand two hours?"

"Sure, Dan." Others spoke up, offered to take a turn.

"All right," the lawman said. "Jack Kennedy will be in the hall 'til mornin'. I'll set up a schedule for the rest of you. If Slattery is in on the kidnappin', he won't leave that room. Anyone tries to reach him, we'll know."

Paul Lutz said. "I'll stand watch, too, Dan. How about the station. Maybe you should be in there after the money is left on the platform."

"No. Let them get the money. I just want that girl safe. There's a lot of land out there. They won't ride far."

"They might have that planned, too," the bartender said. "They didn't miss a thing,

55

tearin' the track up so's you'd be out of town."

Vreeland nodded, slowly. "Danged smart," he said, studying the line of faces in the mirror. "Whoever set things up knew exactly what I'd do. I figure the one who did it had to be smart, just about as clever and careful as a man like Slattery."

Tom Slattery was wiping the soapy water from his chest and shoulders when the knock came on the door. The tension he'd felt when he'd talked to Vreeland had drained slowly from his body as he'd washed, but his tiredness and nerves refused to let him relax completely. He knew what might come if he was kept locked up in here. If Maria died or something violent happened to the girl, the men out there wouldn't give him a chance to prove he was innocent. The four men who had the girl could be doing almost anything. He'd already checked the window that looked out into the back alleyway. It was a two-story drop to the ground; the armed guard spotted at the mouth would cut him down before he got to his feet. He was mulling over a way to get out, racking his brain for an idea, when the knocks made him turn. He dropped the soggy towel into the basin, let his right hand fall to his Colt's butt.

"Yes?"

56

"Thomas. I have your food," Ugo Perani's voice said through the door.

Slattery unlocked the door, stepped aside while the hotel owner passed. The tray he carried held a large T-bone steak, steaming coffee and a half-loaf of home-made Italian bread. The instant Perani set it on the dresser top, he waved Slattery away from the door.

"The deputy will be there all night." He kept his voice lowered. "A man is watching the alley."

Nodding, Slattery said, "How is Maria, Ugo?"

Perani brushed one hand across his bald head. "She is no different." The hand lowered to his mustache, rubbed unconsciously at it. "The doctor is staying . . ." His words died.

"You stay down there with her, Ugo."

"You eat," Ugo said absently. "I know it is what Maria would do for you."

"Thank you, Ugo. Ugo, she'll be all right. She will."

The fat hotelman backed to the door, turned there and gripped the knob. He hesitated without revolving it, looked over his shoulder. "I do not believe you were part of this, Thomas," he said quietly. "Maria would not believe it."

"Ugo . . ."

Shaking his round bald head the hotel owner interrupted. "You cannot stay in here waiting." He let go of the knob, walked back to Slattery. "I know what the men will do."

"I'll be all right, Ugo."

"No, no – you will not. Your horse has been locked in the jail barn. You would be cornered in this room." He stepped to the window, edged the green shade aside and stared toward Boulder Street. "Even if you used a rope, you would be killed before you reached the ground."

Slattery raised his hand and took the pudgy fingers from the shade. "Would you get me a horse?"

"I will. Not as fast and strong as your gelding. But with a head start, you will get away."

"Getting away isn't enough," said Slattery. He inched the shade out, studied the black wall of the general store, fifteen feet across the width of the alley. His eyes traveled from the store roof, recrossed the five yards distance, then stared up at the ceiling overhead. "The roof is right on top, Ugo? There's no attic?"

Perani shook his head, fearfully. "Once you are away from the town, keep riding. I will help only if you leave."

"They'd still believe I set up the kidnapping."

"I do not believe it. Maria will not."

Slattery replaced the edge of the shade. "I'll need a carbine, too. Take the horse out past the homes. South, so I can pick up the tracks. Have it there a half hour before daybreak. Not earlier, though."

Ugo Perani gave no answer for a long minute. Finally, he said, "A horse and a rifle. If you can do nothing, you will leave?"

"I'll do something, Ugo. You think of Maria."

The Italian's round shoulders seemed to slacken. Ugo went to the door, opened it and stepped into the hallway.

Slattery took his shirt from the iron post of the bed and walked to the wall bracket lamp. He doused the wick, then buttoned the sleeves and front while he returned to the window. He reached behind the shade, unlocked the panes. Carefully, easily, he pushed hard on the upper half. The window slid down, but with a low grating noise as the dried wooden surfaces rubbed together.

Slattery pulled his arm away and walked to the dresser. The window was open only a half inch. The sound it gave off would be heard by the guard outside if he did it all at once. He took the knife and sliced into the steak. The time was only eight. He had the entire night to work the window open wide enough for what he meant to do.

Chapter Six

William Hughes got up from the cane-backed chair beside the bed and crossed the small hotel room to the clothes closet. He arched his thin head while he felt into his vest pocket, listening to the chimes of the grandfather clock below in the lobby. "Four," he said to his wife. He checked the time with his watch. "Just right, Edna. It'll be light soon."

Edna Hughes did not answer. She lay as she had lain most of the night and early morning, sleepless, talking only at intervals, and then mostly in anger at him for pacing the room. She had reminded him of just about everything these last nine or ten hours. He'd been the one who'd wanted to see the West. He'd heard about it and had read about the wildness and trouble that writers like Ned Buntline kept pouring into the dime novels. He'd wanted to look the states over for possible shoe factory sites. Well, they had their wildness and trouble. She hadn't even seen a pair of shoes out here. Boots was all she'd seen, and he didn't manufacture boots. He made shoes, and they should have taken a packet from Vera Cruz straight to Boston. Either that or Baltimore. She'd wanted Patricia to see Washington. A visit to the nation's capital would have given the girl something to talk about at home. He understood that and knew, but he'd wanted to come this way, and they had and now it didn't matter what Patricia had seen in Mexico. If they didn't get her back, what did matter . . .

"How long do you think it will take for the money to come?" she asked.

He looked at her, glad to at least have her talk. She seemed so frail and worn and tired on the bed, her face pale against the white pillow. "The message should be to Chamberlain by now. He can wire it to the Fort Worth bank by noon. By afternoon at the latest."

Edna Hughes muffled a sob. "She's all alone with them. What they could do to her."

"Please, Edna."

Her head snapped around to face him. "Don't 'please' me, William Hughes. Don't. Don't! A crime like kidnapping! These are crimes men should never allow! A girl alone with four men! Men who are as brutal as they were to that poor woman downstairs! There

61

should be a penalty so terrible, no one would ever commit that crime! Never! Never!"

"Edna, you'll just make yourself worse."

"It couldn't be worse." Her lips were parted to go on, but instead she sat straight up on the bed. "Did you hear that?" she questioned. She stared at the shaded window.

"I didn't hear anything." William Hughes listened. "No, I didn't hear a thing."

For two full minutes his wife remained silent, not moving, her attention on the window, attempting to again catch the noise she thought had come from the alleyway. Finally, she shook her head. "I was sure I heard something. That man is only three rooms away." She bit her lips together. "William, if we hadn't taken the train, he never would have seen us."

Her husband gave no answer.

"Why? Why, William? Was it so important?"

He returned her stare solemnly. "Edna, I went along with your idea of traveling. I thought then, and I still believe you were right about Patty. But don't blame me. Please, no one is to blame."

Her dark-haired head moved from side to side angrily. "Someone is to blame. That gunman, Slattery." Her voice stopped and she stood quickly, passed the dresser and closet to the window. "There was a noise. I heard it." She threw up the shade, undid the lock. When she tried to push the lower half of the window up, she couldn't. "William, help me. Don't just stand there!"

Hughes was beside his wife. He pushed hard on the window, sent it up and open with the screech of wood against wood.

Below, in the long thin light glare thrown from the window, a town man aimed a rifle at them. He saw it was the Hughes'. He lowered the muzzle.

"What's wrong?" he called. "I didn't know what was happening."

"We thought we heard a noise," William Hughes told him.

"I did hear a noise out there," his wife said emphatically. "There was a noise out there."

Rube Whaleen stiffened where he stood, held the Enfield rifle out in front of him. The Dovers bartender had believed it was Slattery trying to escape from the hotel when he'd heard the window go up. He wished it had been, but now, studying Slattery's room, he could tell his window was shut. The moon, so bright during the early night, was low in the southwest, throwing the wide general store shadow against the hotel. Yet it was clear enough to make out what he needed to see.

Because he stood so quietly he heard the

noise himself at the rear of the alley. He raised the Enfield to hip level, walked deeper into the darkness.

The low scraping was there, ten feet ahead. The bartender's long square jaw tightened, his finger squeezed on the trigger.

A big white cat was at a rubbish bin, trying to drag off some garbage. The brazen cat had heard Whaleen, looked toward him, didn't move.

"Git! Git out!" Whaleen swung the iron barrel at the animal and it scrambled away into the darkness.

Whaleen returned to the light patch beneath the open window. He gestured at the two shadowed faces. "Only a cat," he said, "tryin' to get the rubbish."

"That was a loud noise for a cat," Edna Hughes said.

"It's all it was. Don't worry. I'll be right here. I hear a noise, I'll start shootin'. You got 'nough to worry 'bout."

"Thank you," Mrs. Hughes said.

Rube Whaleen didn't return to the alley mouth right away. He waited until the Hughes' window closed and the shade went down. He stared at Slattery's window, couldn't see a thing. He'd meant what he'd said. He'd open up on Slattery if he got the chance. He'd carried the Enfield through

64

the Shenandoah Valley with Early, and in Petersburg and Farmville, and he knew how to use it. He was just waiting for the chance to use it on Slattery.

Tom Slattery pressed his spine flat against the room wall, watched the alley mouth. The bartender was below him, and Slattery was thankful he'd pushed up the window when he'd heard the Hughes couple make all that noise. His window would open without a sound, he knew. It had taken all night to free the dried wood that much. He'd had it down long enough to stand on the sill and swing his boots up onto the roof. Now, he did not make a motion until the bartender's silhouette was again etched against the street lamps at the end of the alley.

A minute dragged past, then another. Whaleen reached the mouth. Slattery waited five minutes longer before he pulled down on the window.

He walked slowly, carefully. Mr. and Mrs. Hughes wouldn't sleep. The poor people couldn't sleep, not with what they were going through. At any trace of sound he paused, made certain he hadn't been heard.

The moon had almost set by the time he had the window open. He tied around his waist the loose end of the sheet he had secured to the iron post of the bed. He checked on the guard, placed both his feet on the sill and backed upward and outside. If he fell, the sheet would break his fall enough so he had a chance. He'd have to silence the guard without hurting him. But what if the bartender came in shooting?

His stockinged toes gripped the window tops while one hand felt and then gripped the roof edge. Awkwardly, straining every muscle of his arms and chest and shoulders, he pulled himself higher, regretting for the first time in his life his two-hundred-ten pounds.

Panting, every muscle in his long body sore and tired, he worked over the edge, then sprawled out prone on the tar of the flat roof.

The Hughes' shade remained lowered. The guard leaned against the general store clapboards while he smoked a cigarette.

Slattery lay silent and worn out to get his breath. Light faded as the moon set. Thick darkness rose from the prairie, the clearly defined houses and barns and outhouses taking on a fuzzy shading before the blackness engulfed them. Slattery gripped one boot in each hand, crossed the roof to the false-fronted porch in his stockings. He sat while he put on the boots, then he slid down a porch timber and pressed his side hard against the clapboards until he was sure Whaleen hadn't caught the little scrape noises he'd made.

The horse was there behind the out-house of the home at the edge of the prairie. Slattery hadn't heard a sound from the box-like houses as he'd gone past them. He was fifty feet from the tall slim out-building when the man stepped into view. His body was visible vaguely for only a fraction of a moment near the animal making it impossible for Slattery to recognize him.

Slattery jerked the Navy Colt out of his belt, crouched low.

"Tom? Is it you, Tom?" The Italian accent was clear in the night.

"Ugo."

Perani's heavy form led the horse to him. It was a thick-legged palomino with a shortened tail. Even in the dark Slattery could tell he'd give little speed and he doubted the animal's stamina in a long chase. A new Winchester carbine was booted alongside the horn. "He is used mainly for my wagon," Ugo said apologetically. "I do not ride him often, but he knows a saddle. I'm sorry, he's the best I could do." He eyed the revolver in Slattery's hand.

"He's fine, Ugo." Slattery slid the filed-down Colt under his belt, took the bridle. "How is Maria?"

Ugo Perani shrugged, shook his head. "The doctor is a fine man. He sits all night. Mrs. Hughes offered to help." He sighed audibly. "I don't know, Thomas. I can only pray."

"Then she will be all right, Ugo." He paused before he lifted his boot to the stirrup. "It won't help much, I know, Ugo. But I'll bring them in."

The heavy-set hotelman said, "It will help. There must be a penalty." He backed off into the blackness.

Slattery swung solidly into the saddle. The palomino kicked its hind hoofs, jerked up its neck at the strange weight on its back. "Easy. Easy," whispered Slattery. "Easy, boy." He tightened the pull of his right hand, turning the horse, but still allowing the animal to keep its own head. The tracks Lutz and the others had found were less than a mile out. He could travel no further from town than that until there was enough light of daybreak. He had to be positive there was something to track. Despite this mount he couldn't be sure of, he had to chance it. "Easy, boy." He whispered into the animal's ear as the horse walked slowly onto the flat. "You're doing fine. Fine, you're doing fine."

Chapter Seven

Slattery found the tracks when the earliest rays of the sun brightened the horizon east of Rock Spring. He'd dismounted close to three-quarters of a mile from the town, had led the palomino by the bridle while he'd studied the flat for traces of horses's hoofs. Light was coming slowly across the silent prairie when he found what he looked for.

The thick turf had kept the shod-iron shoes from cutting into the ground much, but the wide swath of trampled grass told him the exact area the four had turned off. During the night, he judged, for the gramma grass would have straightened again in the sun. He climbed into the saddle, stared eastward at the blurred spread of land, as yet colorless and grey, darker and with tiny dots of light showing where the town buildings humped up against the growing thin whitish-blue line of morning.

Three minutes passed before he reached the spot where the posse had headed back to help him when they'd heard the gunfire break out.

The grass was barely disturbed ahead, the tracks made by only a single rider. He continued on, finding the trail easy to follow with the horse's slow plodding gait. Four men had taken the Hughes girl. That meant four horses, five if they'd had a mount waiting for her. Four anyway ... The town men led by Lutz had followed only this lone rider. Slattery glanced around. The sun was pushing over the rim of the flat. He didn't have time to backtrack. As soon as it was light enough a guard would notice the open window, if one hadn't already. The palomino was too slow to chance letting a lawman as careful and capable as Vreeland get close to him. He had to depend on the fact the man he followed would eventually turn and head for the place the girl had been taken.

He rode on, bent low alongside the horse's thick neck, sitting easier now that the animal was used to him, but continually giving backward glances to see if anyone was behind him. Gradually, the sky turned clean and clear blue and the broad length of prairie was touched with flame.

Two miles further on he caught sight of the tops of the trees to the northwest, then the first mesquite thicket stretching out northward beyond the river. Slattery felt the heat of the sun on his shoulders. He knew what the kidnappers had done even before he reached the stream.

The group had split, each going in different directions to lead off the posse. The ruse had worked. This man had headed directly for this creek that fed off the Colorado somewhere above him around San Saba. He'd gone into the water amid a copse of moss-hung water oaks spotted with hackberry. There wasn't a sign of a hoof print for two hundred yards north or south on either bank. Slattery pulled in to allow the palomino a drink before returning to the growing heat of the flat.

North and east were towns, less than twenty miles, he'd judge. He knew the land clear to the gentle, rolling cow country of Choctaw Flats. Northwest the mesquite thickets stretched out for miles, tall cactuses rising up in spots among the twisted thorny trees. West, beyond the Llano and San Saba, the rougher, brushier terrain ran clear to the Comanche country of the Staked Plains.

Slattery chose the southwest. Small ranches spotted the country, and no matter how little the spreads were, they had the buildings the men needed to hide the Hughes girl ... Sun raised a thin whitish mist over the water. He kneed the palomino along the shallow channel, his eyes switching from side to side, studying the banks to find the spot where a horse had come out.

71

Dan Vreeland sat up on the cell bunk he'd used as a bed for the night. His small thin face was calm, relaxed below his mussed hair while he pulled on his boots.

"Why didn't you look up before now?" he asked Rube Whaleen. "You could've seen the window was open ten, fifteen minutes ago."

"I didn't think, Dan," the bartender said angrily. "It's my fault. Such a damned stupid thing to do."

"Have Tracy get my horse ready." The lawman took his gunbelt from the chair beside the bunk. He straightened and buckled on the heavy closed-flap holster.

"I'm goin' with you," Whaleen said.

"No. I go alone. I can handle this alone."

The long square face shook from side to side. Whaleen rubbed at his stubbed jaw. "I let him get out. I go, Dan. I've got to live in this town."

The sheriff walked past him through the cell block corridor and into the small jail office. He did not speak while he chose a long-barreled Henry rifle from the racked guns. He opened the lower drawer of his roll top desk and took out a box of .44 shells.

Whaleen watched the lawman load the weapon. "I come, Dan."

"All right. Get the horses. Stop at my house

and tell Rosie I'm goin' out. She'll put up some grub for us."

Dan Vreeland inserted the last cartridge into the chamber, then he left the office and crossed Boulder straight to the Sorento House alleyway. He'd underestimated Slattery, but he wouldn't again. He'd let the man keep the Navy Colt he had shoved under his belt because, for some reason, he'd half-believed Slattery was telling the truth. He had no doubt now, about Slattery and about his job here in Rock Spring. Election time was coming again this Fall. The county wasn't going to re-elect a lawman who'd allowed a man to escape as easily as Slattery had. He had a wife and three young ones . . . Dan Vreeland turned into the alley, his own self-anger stronger than Whaleen's had been, driving him on so he knew exactly what he'd do.

Ugo Perani and William Hughes stood halfway along the length of the building, their eyes on the top of the open window.

Hughes spoke as soon as he saw the Henry rifle. "Sheriff, you're not going after them?"

"Slattery'll leave a trail," Vreeland said flatly.

Hughes glanced high at the third window beyond the one Slattery had used for his escape. "We're paying the money, Sheriff.

73

Please don't do anything. My wife . . ."

"Mr. Hughes," the lawman cut in, "I've got a track to follow. And a man. I'm bringing him in, tied over a saddle or sittin'. I don't care which."

"Sheriff, please."

Vreeland's voice softened. "This way's a better chance for your daughter, Mr. Hughes. A posse would be seen. One, two men have a better chance."

Ugo Perani said, "I know Slattery. He is not bad, Sheriff. If you give him a chance." His words fell off at Vreeland's hard stare.

"Keepin' him in that room was givin' him a chance, Ugo." He swung on his heel, headed into the street.

Rube Whaleen, a flour-sack bulging with food in his hands, ran past the cottonwoods and water oak of the square. A boney, stoop-shouldered man led Vreeland's stallion and a second horse through the livery work area. Neither man had reached Vreeland when Paul Lutz appeared from the high livery barn doorway, already mounted on a long-legged grey mare.

Vreeland climbed into the saddle, waited for Lutz to reach them.

Paul Lutz held his heavy double-barreled Greener shotgun in his left hand, the reins in his right.

"Two of us are enough," Vreeland said. "This ain't a posse."

"I'm goin' after Slattery whether I ride with you or not," the station agent answered. "Dan, I was the man who talked Slattery into carrying the bags from the train."

"No. There'll be messages come in 'bout the reward money. You'll have to be here to handle them."

"The train conductor is takin' that for me, Dan. He works a key," Lutz gazed along the length of the street, let his eyes rest on the lines of buildings. "I've heard the talk, Dan. They wonder about me in this, some of them. I was at the station. The station is bein' used as the delivery place for the ransom. I don't look good. This is my town, too, Dan."

Vreeland looked at the station agent thoughtfully, then at Whaleen. "Okay, the three of us go."

He nodded down to the hostler. "Thanks, Tracy. Tell Jack Kennedy he takes over my office. Tell him no one follows us."

"Yuh, sure, Dan."

Sheriff Vreeland kneed his stallion, pulled ahead of the other two riders. "We spread out 'til we find his trail," he said over his shoulder. "The one who does fires once into the air. But that's all the firin' we do 'til we

75

close in. Save every bullet you have for when you need them."

Rube Whaleen nodded, stared past the residential section, his square unshaven face deadly serious. Paul Lutz slapped the pocket of his coat, bulging with No. 10 buckshot shells. "I've got plenty, Dan," he said tightly. "I've got enough to blow Slattery apart, to give him exactly what he deserves."

Chapter Eight

The single shot ahead came as a shock to Slattery.

He swung the palomino to the right, off the sandbar into the cover of the thick-trunked oaks. His coat unbuttoned, he had the Colt clear of his belt. Then, at the banging of the next two shots, he jammed the revolver back into place.

The boy doing target practice stood back to Slattery. He was tall and lanky, with a mass of uncut blonde hair. The ancient iron coffee pot he used as a target still sat on the rock in the middle of the river bed. The boy turned when he heard the palomino break through the brush onto the bank. He was about eighteen, but his skin and body were already tough and hard from his life and work on the Texas flat. His home, a small log and adobe house with a larger log barn behind it, sat lonely and squat a mile west. Beyond the buildings Slattery counted four head of cattle in the rolling, endless swells of grass, dotted here and there sparsely by mesquite that stretched to the blue-brown line of the horizon.

"Mornin'," Slattery said easily.

"Mornin'," the boy answered. He held the old Springfield barrel-down, grinned at Slattery. "You scared me comin' up quiet like that."

Slattery laughed. "Havin' much luck?"

"No. I can't get the hang of it. Rifle kicks to the left since it's been converted." He looked at the dry wooden stock. "My pa had it in the war, and he and Ma won't let me practice 'less I'm clear of the house and the young 'uns." He gestured toward the ranch. "Why don't you go over and set a spell. Pa'll be glad. We don't see many people livin' this far from town."

Slattery let the palomino drink. He could feel the horse tiring under him, even though they had been moving for only a little more than an hour. At the house, three, four young children played in the yard, running back and forth and around the adobe well. He couldn't stop at every ranch, and he'd seen no sign that the men he followed had left the river yet. He didn't believe the kids would be running and yelling like that if Patricia Hughes was being held in one of the buildings.

"Obliged," Slattery said. "But I better keep ridin'. Got to be in San Antone tomorrow." He nodded at the Springfield. "Try pressin' harder into your shoulder. Aim an inch or so to the right 'til you control the kick."

The boy aimed at the target and squeezed the trigger. The coffee pot leaped with the impact of the bullet, tumbled in an arc, and splashed into the water.

The boy grinned at Slattery and Slattery grinned back. "Thanks. Thanks, mister," he said happily while Slattery swung his mount. The boy's boots kicked up large bomb-bursts of water as he ran to retrieve his target.

Eight miles further southwest, Slattery struck the next ranch. Like the first, the house was of log and adobe, the barn all log, the greyish wood of each building just as sunbaked and weather dry. Slattery spoke softly to the palomino while he turned into the willows, batting mosquitoes with his hat. As absently, he took a good look behind him. Nothing moved in the shimmering mid-morning heat haze. Nothing showed along the river bank.

A thin man, naked to the waist, was in the open barn doorway greasing the spoked wheels of a small farm wagon. He stared around when he heard the horse's hoofs. He straightened, spat a mouthful of tobacco juice and watched Slattery enter his yard.

Slattery visibly gave his attention to the man while he approached the barn, yet he did not allow his eyes to leave the house. The rancher's hands were black with grease, his long face veined and tight to the bone. If the girl was here and the man was drawing the palomino in, he'd be no trouble, not with hands slippery like that. When Slattery saw the woman step through the house doorway, he knew Patricia wasn't here.

The infant the woman rocked in her arms couldn't be more than a month old. The woman was young and pretty, her bosom large under her gingham dress. She didn't smile at Slattery, simply followed her husband's stride to meet the horse.

"Been travelin' all night from Coleman," Slattery said. He made no motion to dismount, kept both hands on the saddle horn. "I'd like to rub and grain my horse. I'd be glad to pay you."

"Sure thing," the rancher said. He was

close to fifty, probably twenty years older than his wife. "Always glad to have people stop in." He turned to his wife who smiled now, happy in the thought that she and her husband would have someone to talk to. "Get coffee and biscuits, Weezy. Man likes a bite when he's been ridin' so long."

Slattery almost missed seeing the third ranch beyond the east bank. About nine-thirty he'd passed due west of Rock Spring, eighteen, twenty miles out. He'd stayed fifteen minutes at the Slowey ranch, too long if he was being followed. If he judged Vreeland right, the lawman was after him. Now, Slattery no longer stayed in the middle of the stream. The palomino was too slow. On the bank he made better time, but Slattery had to chance the fact his men would leave the water and head west.

He saw only the barn at first through the screen of willows and cottonwoods. The small low-built structure had a corral of willow poles on its near side, and that was all there seemed to be.

Slattery turned the palomino down the bank, allowed the tired horse to pick its own way across and up the higher opposite bank.

Once he was clear of the brush he saw the soddy a homesteader had built against a small rise of land. The house had been dug into the low hill like a gopher hole, with a roof of willow poles that barely showed.

Slattery rode slowly, glanced behind him to check the snakey tree-lined creek and empty prairie. Five mossy horns grazed near the barn which was constructed of new wood. Cottonwood fuzz, drifted over the sunscorched grass and meadow larks sang, the single sound except for the horse's hoofs plodding toward the closed soddy doorway.

"Dammit, that's who it is," Joe Paxton said, peering past the dirty cardboard that covered the soddy's single window. "He's comin' from the north, Baine. You see that?"

"He couldn't've tracked me, Joe," answered Baine. "He's still north. I didn't leave the creek 'til I was a mile below him. If he found us, it wasn't me, Joe."

"He tracked you," Al Fox cut in, his voice tight and irritated. "He back tracked, damn him. To make it look like he's just ridin' in." He straightened where he stood behind Paxton under the hanging overhead oil lamp. He rubbed his flat jaw, then unconsciously, habitually, adjusted the twin six-guns thonged down to his black trouser legs. "He doesn't know me, Joe. I c'n step out and bust him before he's off that horse."

Paxton muttered a curse. "That's all we'd need, shootin'. You think he'd be alone? One shot and we'd have whoever is with him on our necks. We'd never get out of this stinkhole." He looked around to the closed door at the rear of the wide mud-walled room. A table and three chairs were the only furniture, set midway between the door and the open stone fireplace. "Milo, get out there, you and your woman."

The door opened instantly. A big man, getting so paunchy his belt hung under his belly, stepped into the room. His jowly face was heavily lined and sallow, his black hair streaked with premature grey. Milo Gann's wife was her husband's age, forty. She still had traces of her youthful beauty, but she'd hidden it under the men's clothing she wore, in her husband's jeans and too-large faded green shirt, with a bandanna around her neck. The man in the doorway behind her stared at Paxton. He said, "You want me to go out the roof hole, Joe?"

"You stay in with the girl, Allerby. Keep her quiet."

The door closed.

"He's almost here," Baine said. He glanced at Paxton, his smooth beardless face concerned and cautious. "He can't come in, Joe."

"He won't," Paxton told him. And to Milo Gann, "Get out and talk to him. See he moves on."

Gann's pasty features showed fear. "Suppose he won't. He followed Baine's tracks, he knows you're here."

"That's right," Fox agreed. "He's alone. We oughta bust him, Joe. We get him inside, no shot'll be heard."

Flora Gann said, "There wasn't to be any killing." She faced her husband. "Milo, Lutz promised no killing when . . ."

Joe Paxton grabbed the woman's arm, twisted it so she doubled over, ready to scream. Paxton's other hand covered her mouth. He stared up at Milo Gann, his eyes sharp and sure and threatening. "You wanted the money, Gann. You get out there. Invite him in for a bite. We'll do the rest."

Chapter Nine

Slattery wondered about this small spread, mainly about the new barn. Whoever owned it and the soddy certainly hadn't made a go of the place. Chances were that he wouldn't, the way the land to the south was wind-blown into sandy, dry washes and patches of alkali. There was only spotty grass beyond river's drinking distance, and behind the building it was too sandy to make even farming worthwhile. Slattery watched for hoofprints that came from the river. He saw none. He was fifty feet from the soddy when the door opened and a big, dirty-looking man stepped through the sunken doorway into sight.

The man hesitated an instant just beyond the doorway. Then, as though he'd suddenly noticed Slattery, he walked forward into the hot bright sunlight. He waved one hand in a friendly gesture.

"Mornin'," he said. "You lookin' for work?"

Slattery reined in. "Not work, thanks," he answered. "My horse picked up a stone under one shoe. I was hopin' you'd have somethin' in your barn I could fix it with."

"I reckon I have." The rancher kept hesitating, as though he tried to find the exact words he wanted to say. Watching him, Slattery didn't miss the small twitch at the corner of his left eye, nor how the man tried to control it. "Here, I'll handle your horse. My woman's got coffee inside." He lifted both hands to take the bridle. "We don't get a chance to get to town. People don't ride out this way."

84

Slattery dismounted on the right side where the Winchester was booted. "Thanks, but your forge'll be enough. I didn't mean . . ."

"I'm glad to do it." He walked along beside Slattery, brushed one hand through his greying hair. "Look, you go on in and have that coffee. My woman'll be glad to see someone to talk to."

They were even with the doorway, Slattery leading the palomino out wide from the window, the rancher almost blocking the soddy from his view. Slattery shifted his step, not sure whether the man he hunted was in the barn or the soddy. The rancher's arm stayed high, the hand moving as though he intended to grip the bridle. The fingers curved into a fist that swung back at Slattery's jaw.

Slattery jerked his head aside, clear of the blow. He let go of the bridle and moved in on the rancher. The miss left the man standing facing Slattery awkwardly, both hobnailed boots planked solidly on the ground. Slattery swung out with his open left hand, caught the jaw bone directly under the ear, knocking the man sprawling in the direction of the barn.

The palomino stomped and yanked up its head, shying away from the men. As the animal moved aside, the rancher pushed

85

himself onto his hands and knees and scrambled like a terrified, wounded dog for the house.

He was on his feet now, both hands out, reaching for Slattery's booted carbine.

Slattery stepped toward him, his right hand on the butt of his Navy Colt. "Hold it, mister. Don't."

"You hold it! Stop right there!"

The words came from behind him in the doorway of the soddy. Joe Paxton stood half in and half out of the room with a six-gun in each hand. Slattery turned fast, heard the first, then the second low sharp click of the hammers.

"Drop it!" Paxton said, his eyes on the Colt.

Slattery's fingers loosened on the Colt's handle. The weapon fell to the ground, kicked up a small puff of dust when it struck.

Slattery hadn't taken his eyes from Paxton. His lips opened to speak, shut again as Milo Gann's doubled fist slammed him from behind, catching him flush in the nape of the neck.

Before Slattery began to go down, Paxton moved toward him. Gann stood over the unconscious man, the Winchester he'd pulled from the leather boot raised in his hand to smash the iron barrel against Slattery's head.

"Cut that," Paxton snapped. "Cut it!"

"He hit me! No man hits me! Not like that, he don't!"

"Cut it, I said." Paxton shoved the carbine aside, pushed Gann toward the palomino. "We stand out here, anyone else with him'll see. Get that horse into the barn." He bent over Slattery, brushed his hand across Slattery's chest, then down along his side to check for a hide-out gun. He glanced at Gann. "Move, damn you. Move." His stare shifted to the river, scanned the brush and timber along Hackberry Creek. He couldn't see any more riders, but he was sure this man hadn't left Rock Spring alone. "Fox, Baine," he called over his shoulder, "give me a hand with him. Hurry up."

Fox and Baine ran from the soddy. Paxton had Slattery by the arms, was dragging him to the door. Fox took one arm, Allerby the feet.

"He's a big son," Baine said. "Know him?"

"Name's Slattery," said Joe Paxton. "He's the one who fought Concho."

"He can tell us why Conch didn't ride out this mornin'," Fox said. He lowered his head, passed backwards through the doorway into the damp-smelling dark room. "Damn him if anythin' happened to Conch."

"Right here," Paxton said. He dropped

87

Slattery onto the dirt floor. He took Slattery's Colt and laid it on the stone fireplace mantle. Then, he swung around to study the river and flat again. Still no sign of a living thing out there. Milo Gann, puffing and wheezing from his short trot from the barn, reached the sunken doorway.

"Horse's all locked up, Joe," he panted.

"There are still tracks to cover," Paxton said. "Let your own horse out of the stall. Then haze that cattle in close to the barn. Run one or two around the house here. Keep them movin' so they'll cover any hoofprints."

Milo Gann's jowly head nodded. He pulled at the belt below his sagging belly. "Flora," he called in through the doorway. "I want a hand, Flora."

Paxton swore at him. "Do it alone. Anyone is out there, make it look like you're just workin' your spread." He lowered his head, backed into the soddy while he gave the empty prairie and river timber one final look. "Baine," he said suddenly. "Get that palomino out again and ride south along the river."

Baine said, "Anyone ridin' in'll see, Joe. They'll track me."

"That's exactly what we want," answered Paxton. "His tracks lead in here. You'll make them lead out. Keep goin' far enough before

88

you double back. Just make sure you throw off anyone trackin' that palomino."

"He's comin' 'round," Al Fox said, his head and wide shoulders leaning forward while he watched Slattery. "I'll tie him, Joe."

Slattery heard the words that seemed to come to him from a long, long distance. He opened his eyes, rolled onto his elbows. A sharp hot pain slashed across the nape of his neck and drove up into his head. The two men who stood over him, blocking out the lamplight, he'd never seen before. One was a trifle shorter than the other dressed in black, but both were cut from the same die, no softness in their lean, hard-boned faces, their toughness and cruelty ingrained and deep. A third and fourth pair of trousered legs stood near a table. The man was younger than these two, his cheeks and jaw smooth and beardless. The woman dressed in man's shirt and jeans, surprised Slattery. He hadn't expected a woman. "Let him come 'round," he heard Paxton say. "I want to know what to expect."

"He can tell us 'bout Conch," said the one in black. Two guns, Slattery noted, both were double gun rigs. "I'll make him tell."

"Don't touch him, Fox," another male voice said from the rear of the darkly shadowed room. Through an open doorway, Slattery saw the fourth man. He was as lean as Paxton, stubby, blocking the doorway with the easy, hip-shot slouch of a rider. A Winchester carbine was in his right hand. Beyond the weapon, curled up in the hazy lamplight on a cotlike bed was Patricia Hughes. Her stare was frozen on Slattery, terrified at what could happen.

"Look, Allerby," Al Fox snarled. "Conch's my kin. Anythin' happened to him, I want to know. He come from that town, he knows what went on." He bent, grabbed Slattery's shoulder to pull him to his feet. "You fought Concho, Slattery. Why didn't he ride out here this mornin'?"

Joe Paxton said, "That can wait, Fox. Drop it!"

"The hell I will."

"You damnwell will. This one didn't come out alone. I want to know how many others are with him." There was no pretense in Paxton's voice or stare. He shifted his stance, stretching both legs and his big right arm while he moved, his hand inches from his six-gun. His expression had changed, making him seem almost sleepy. "He answers me."

Al Fox's eyes flicked from Paxton's hand to Allerby in the doorway. Fox made a gesture of disgust. "Ahh!" he grunted angrily. He whirled on his bootheel and stalked to the small window. Removing the cardboard, he looked outside.

"You didn't come alone," Joe Paxton said to Slattery. "How many more are with you?"

"I am alone. That thumper you put on me did his job so well, the law at Rock Spring locked me in the hotel because they believed I was part of taking that girl."

Paxton studied him. "So, you got away and figured we'd let you in on it?"

Fox swung around at the window. "Oh, hell, Joe. You can see how much of a bluff . . ."

"I can see I'm handlin' this like I want. You shut up, Fox. Right now, you shut."

The woman dressed in men's clothes edged away from the table, clear of the men. In the quiet of the room the clomping of hoofs was close outside, sounding to Slattery as though cattle were being driven past the soddy. Slattery didn't move. He watched Fox again turn away from Paxton.

Paxton's voice lowered, became almost friendly. "You figured you were in trouble anyway, so you'd throw in with us?"

Slattery said flatly, "I got out to find you and take that girl back to her parents." He let his eyes shift to Patricia Hughes, huddled

91

on the bunk, now straining to listen. "That's what I mean to do."

"And you got clear by yourself and rode here all alone. Jest like that you make a damn fool of Vreeland."

Allerby chuckled in the doorway. "I ain't yet seen the man who can fool Vreeland when he's right in town. We had to tear up half mile of rail to get him out. You just walked out of that hotel."

"I got out," Slattery said quietly. He looked directly at Paxton. "I spent as much time as your man did hiding my tracks in the creek."

Fox said, "If you ask me, they'll be a posse along damn soon. This one comes in ahead to draw us out. I don't like it, Joe."

"I don't either," agreed Allerby. The carbine barrel came up slowly. "I say we finish him, Joe. There's enough room in that barn for us and the horses."

"Keep that down," Paxton said. "A shot'd be heard out there. We can't be in the open, not with a chance of someone watchin' from them trees." He motioned to Slattery. "Into the back room, you."

Slattery took a step past him. He spotted the ancient muzzle-loading rifle then, leaned barrel-up against the far side of the fireplace. His own Navy Colt was on the mantle.

"No you don't," Fox said. "You were in Rock Spring. What happened to Concho Grady?" He came past Joe Paxton who made no attempt to stop him. "You had reason to jump Conch."

"He rode out of town after the fight," Slattery answered. "You must've had a plan for that, you planned everything else right down to the minute. You tell me."

Fox's sharp eyes burned into Slattery. He rubbed his jaw. Finally he nodded at the doorway.

Slattery walked past Allerby into the small bedroom. A home-made unpainted cottonwood dresser was set against the wall opposite the bed. The only other item of furniture was a hide-bottomed chair, as old and in need of repairs as the bureau. Patricia Hughes hadn't changed position where she was huddled. Her body shook silently, and he knew she was fighting not to cry. Her hands held her black skirt pulled down over her knees almost desperately, as though somehow she was safer as long as her legs and body stayed hidden beneath her clothing.

"Did they hurt you?" Slattery asked softly.

The girl shook her head, biting her lower lip and not looking at Allerby who spoke quickly from the doorway.

"Shut up. No talk." He jerked the

93

Winchester muzzle at the chair. "You just sit there."

Slattery sat, letting his lips crack in a smile at the girl. She did not return the smile, simply remained tense and silent. She's been like that all the time, he thought, realizing how terrible it must have been and was for her. He'd stay quiet and let her get hold of herself. If they both gave no trouble, later they might be allowed to talk. He surveyed the room. A hole had been cut at the back of the roof. It was covered over with wood and probably sod outside, but it was a second exit from the house ... He could see no others, not in here anyway. The voices of the gunmen droned in the other room, their conversation low and guarded. Allerby had stepped in with them, yet he'd spotted himself where he could look at both the bed and the chair.

Slattery said in a low whisper. "Patricia, they didn't touch you?"

"No. Don't talk, please," she said, "Allerby and Fox." She stared wide-eyed at the doorway, stiffening along her entire body.

Allerby leaned back on his heels where he stood, looked in at them. He watched for a long, drawn-out minute before he returned his attention to what Paxton was saying.

"Your father is paying the money," Slattery said softly to Patricia.

She bit her lip tighter, made white thin lines at the corners of her mouth. "It won't matter. I know what they're going to do. I heard them. Please, don't make it come sooner."

She huddled her knees closer to her chest, stared blankly ahead.

Slattery studied her. If she'd had any hope, he'd destroyed it when he'd been taken by these men.

She accepted what would come, it was in the sound of her voice. Even if he did get a chance to break away, she'd be of no help, not like this. Considering that, he took papers and a tobacco sack from the pocket of his dust-streaked grey shirt. He spun a cigarette into shape. He was striking a match when the outside soddy door banged the dirt wall and Milo Gann ran in.

"Riders comin'," he called shrilly. "Three of them, I see, Paxton! Slattery said he was alone!"

Fox cursed wildly. A chair scuffed the dirt and bounced back against the wall as Fox loomed up in the bedroom doorway.

"You, damn you," the gunman spat. "You talked so damn quiet, and you led them right here."

95

Patricia Hughes' eyes were closed tight, her body huddled even more trying to make herself smaller and not a part of this. Allerby, Winchester aimed, was beside Fox. Slattery sat absolutely still, the cigarette between his lips, his eyes on the carbine muzzle and the twin six-guns a fraction of an inch from Fox's fingertips.

"It's Sheriff Vreeland," the woman's voice said at the window. "Whaleen from the saloon is with him. And Paul Lutz."

"Take him," Joe Paxton said. He moved fast past Fox and Allerby into the bedroom. Allerby was right alongside him, quickly.

"Up," Allerby said, jabbing the carbine barrel deep into Slattery's side. He twisted the long solid steel. It dug along the rib line, driving the air from Slattery's lungs as he stood and went with the gunmen.

Fox and Paxton peered through the window. Slattery halted behind them.

"Are there any more of them?" Paxton asked Slattery. "How many?"

"I don't know. I thought I'd covered . . ."

"You didn't cover anythin'," Paxton said. "You'll stand right in here. They try to get in, you get it first. Then the girl." And to Milo Gann, "Get out and make it look like you're workin'. Keep them off."

Gann pulled at his thick jowls. "I don't know 'bout Vreeland. I didn't fool Slattery, I won't fool him."

"I'll go out with him," said Flora Gunn. She gripped the doorlatch. "They'd expect the two of us together, Milo. I'll go."

Paxton nodded. "Vreeland tries to look in here or the barn, both of you duck. We got clear aim through the window." He pushed Slattery to the left, flush against the wall. "Not one move, you. Stay put and shut or you get it before them out there."

Chapter Ten

Paul Lutz had hung behind Sheriff Vreeland and Whaleen since the three riders had left the creek bed. During the late morning, when they'd stopped to rest their horses, dismounting to eat and walk, stretching their legs and arms, Whaleen had come up with the idea that they branch off in three directions and meet below the creek bend twenty miles south. Lutz had kept out of the discussion, had chewed on the tasteless sandwiches Vreeland's wife had put up. The beef was stringy and had turned soft and lardy within the saddlebag, giving it a tongue-drying dustiness. Whaleen had started to gripe that they'd never catch Slattery. He believed it would be better to head back to town and wait for him and the rest of the kidnappers to come in for the reward money. Lutz had kept out of that, too. Later on, when everything which was said and done was mulled over and talked to death, he wasn't going to have one act or statement pointing to him. The main thing now was to keep behind the lawman. Slattery's tracks led up to Gann's soddy, but Lutz had absolutely no idea of what had happened there. If trouble did break, it would be a simple matter to empty both Greener barrels into Vreeland and Whaleen before either could turn around.

"There's Gann and his wife," Rube Whaleen said. "Maybe they know somethin' comin' out like that."

Dan Vreeland said, "Move out ten feet on each side. Don't give a single target in case he is here."

Lutz nicked his horse's flanks with his spurs, made the animal move faster. Once abreast of the lawman, he slowed to Vreeland's stallion's long-legged gait. Paxton and the others would be watching, would hear every word, ready to open up if they had to. The cattle which fed on the bunch grass was typical of Gann, who was known for running his homestead sloppily. The barn was his price for allowing the girl to be held here. Lutz had chosen his man right. Eight hundred dollars was all it had cost. And he'd end up with fifty thousand of the reward money. He'd planned this right down to the light of the moon tonight. Now, as he drew his horse up and in a line with Vreeland and Whaleen, he rested the shotgun flat across the horn, not chancing a single thing.

"Sheriff. Wal, how are you?" Milo Gann said, his thick-cheeked face bright with a smile. "Rube, Lutz, glad to see you. Come in and sit a spell."

"We've trailed a rider from Rock Spring," Vreeland told him. "His tracks led here."

"A drifter was here," Gann said. "He stopped and had coffee with me and Flora."

His wife nodded, her smile of welcome as wide as her husband's. "His name was Slattery. He stayed long enough for two cups." The smile faded. "What did he do, Sheriff?"

Vreeland told them about the kidnapping, ending with, "He was in on the whole setup, and I want him. I figured maybe I track him long enough, he'll lead us to the others."

Flora Gann shivered, gripped her elbows together across her chest and rubbed them

99

nervously. "And, he was here. He was so quiet, Sheriff. You're sure he was the one?"

"He was the one," said Vreeland. He stared along the ground at the confusion of hoof prints.

Milo Gann said, "He went past the barn, Sheriff, toward the crick, Sheriff. I was goin' into town today. You don't think I better not leave my woman here alone?"

"I don't think he'll be back," Vreeland told him. He flicked his wrist and his stallion started off.

Milo Gann took a few hasty steps alongside the animal. "You're sure you don't want to come in and have coffee? All of you?"

"We can't take the time," Paul Lutz said while he passed the side of the soddy. Then, as if an afterthought, he called over his shoulder in a higher, clear voice. "You do see this Slattery, don't give him a chance, Milo. He killed one of his own gang named Grady in Rock Spring. Watch out for him."

Fox muttered an obscene curse, brought up his right hand and stepped toward Slattery. "You rotten liar. You killed Concho! You!"

"Don't. Don't, you fool," Joe Paxton warned. "Get back. Make noise now, Vreeland'll have us cornered in here."

"He killed Conch," Fox said hatefully.

100

He'd halted, let both hands drop to his low-slung holstered six-guns. "I'll fix him. I'll damnwell fix him."

"You don't now," ordered Paxton. "Not yet. That Vreeland'll hear a shot. You don't do anything that'll spoil it."

"He's mine though. I finish Slattery, Joe."

Allerby, with the Winchester still leveled at the window hadn't moved. He spoke quietly. "Joe, that's Al's right. Conch was his kin and it's his right." Then he glanced at the door opening inward and added in the same tone, "Milo'll have to find out how the reward's comin' in. We gotta know if that town's gettin' ready for us."

Joe Paxton nodded. "Inside the back room," he said to Slattery. He stood between Fox and Slattery while Slattery moved into the bedroom. Milo Gann and his wife came through the doorway. "Stay outside," Paxton told the woman. "Make sure they keep ridin'."

Flora Gann hesitated, looked at her husband.

"Out," Paxton said irritatedly. "Gann, you tell her. I don't like the way she's been hangin' back since we brought the girl."

"We didn't agree on any killin'," Flora began.

Milo interrupted. "Shut your mouth, Flora. Do what he says."

The woman studied her husband for a moment, her face doubtful. Milo turned on her. "Get out there! Do what you're told!" His hand had doubled into a fist and his immense belly jounced up and down as he stepped toward her. "Do it, Flora!"

Without a word, she left the soddy. Paxton said, "You control her, Gann, or I will." He continued to keep his glance on Fox, but he went on to Milo Gann," Give them ten minutes and hitch your rig. You'll go into Rock Spring and find out what's been done. I don't want us ridin' into any trap tonight."

"You think I'd better go in with him?" Allerby said.

Joe Paxton's head shook back and forth. "They're used to seein' him drive in alone. It has to look the same as always." His whiskered face shifted to Fox. "We don't leave until he's back with the word there's no trap."

Fox didn't seem to be listening. He said. "I take care of Slattery." Habitually, unconsciously, he hitched up his double gun rig. "That's first for me, Joe. I don't ride 'til I finish him."

Paxton nodded slowly. "He's yours then. When we're ready to go."

Slattery sat on the chair. He'd wanted to go closer to Patricia Hughes and talk to her, but it went through his mind that she was as afraid of talking to him as she was of the men in the other room. From the close hot stuffiness of the room, he could feel it was just about noon, with the sun directly overhead. The hide carpet in one corner gave off a sour stench. He watched the girl, sitting as she had before, her eyes open but seemingly unaware he was present.

He lit another cigarette, grateful at least they hadn't touched the girl. Maybe the presence of Gann's wife had caused that. Maybe ... Five, almost six hours to sunset. Gann would be back by then. Paxton and the rest wouldn't budge from the soddy. They weren't worried about his getting away, hadn't even bothered to tie him or the girl. He studied the ceiling. He'd get about far enough to push the hole open and wham. Maybe Paxton would use a knife, but Fox and Allerby would shoot to kill. Fox worried him, yet there was no way he could hit the man first, and he inhaled long on the cigarette, slowly, to make himself relax. He had to think this out. He had the girl to consider. She'd been his responsibility since the instant the fight started with Concho

Grady. Not for one moment had he doubted that.

He heard her move and he leaned nearer to her. "You'll be all right," he said quietly. "They'll get you to your parents tonight."

Her small face was drawn, wide-eyed as she shook her head. "What'll he do, shoot you?" she asked.

Slattery grinned at the incongruous question. "Not if I can help it."

That didn't help. She bit her lips tight. "You shouldn't have come. I've caused this. Everything . . ." She lowered her face and shook her head. "I never do anything right."

"This isn't your fault." He touched her hand, made her look at him. "It isn't. The gang had everything planned right up to your leaving the train."

"No. It's my fault. We wouldn't have been in Mexico if I was what I should be. We wouldn't have been on that train."

She's scared, Slattery thought, but not just because of what had happened. He recollected the smile she'd given him on the train, how unsure she'd been when he'd left her and her parents at the Sorento House. She didn't know how to talk to him even now, not really. She's so plain, but there was something about her face and chin, clean-cut and smooth and nice. Her hair, if it wasn't drawn back into a bun, would fall soft and loose about her shoulders. He felt sorry for her, not only because of the danger. There was something he didn't understand, though he knew it had little to do with sympathy . . .

The Gann woman had returned to the soddy, and she was lighting the small fireplace. A kitchen pan banged the andiron while she prepared something to eat.

Slattery listened for a moment to the low drone of talk around the table.

"Everyone is inside," he said softly. "Can you run fast enough to keep up with me getting to the barn?"

"Please, I couldn't . . ."

"You could, Patricia. They'll be eating soon. Not one of them has even looked in here. They've got their horses hidden in the barn, and only one of them has his carbine with him. That means at least three carbines with the horses."

She looked at him, her eyes wide with the anxiety and hope in what he was saying. The smell of steak and beans was strong, good.

"That hole in the roof's there so Gann'll have another way out. Dirt'll be over it, but a good shove, and I'll have it opened."

"It might work," she said. "It will."

"Once I get it open, I'll push you through. Run as fast as you can for the barn. Don't worry about me. I'll make it. But if I don't, lock yourself in and start shooting. Vreeland can't be too far off."

Her hope changed to terror. "I can't fire a gun. I don't know how."

"There'll be time for me to explain. Quiet now." He leaned forward so he was off the rawhide seat. Carefully, inch by inch, he shifted the chair to a spot directly beneath the chopped out section of roof. He sat again, too far from Patricia to talk. No one came to the door in the ten minutes which passed before Flora Gann dished out the steak and beans.

The men were all at the table, their talk kept low.

Flora Gann called out to the bedroom. "I'll bring something in to you."

Joe Paxton said, "They don't eat. The weaker she is, the less trouble she'll give us."

Slattery watched Patricia Hughes. Her fright was there, but the hope was also. He let a minute drag by, another. Then he rose slowly, hugged the wall. He was standing straight, both hands raised high above his head, the fingertips touching the board which blocked the roof opening.

Patricia gasped, "No!" and with the word came the unmistakable click of a six-gun being cocked.

"Go ahead," said Joe Paxton in the

doorway. "Try it, Slattery. One push, you give me reason to chop you down."

Chapter Eleven

Sheriff Dan Vreeland called a halt five miles southwest of the Gann homestead. "Let the horses drink," he told Whaleen and Lutz. "I've got the spot where he turned back east."

He held his mount on the low bank of the creek until the others had pushed through the willows on the opposite side and down onto a tongue of sandbar that rose above the lazy current. Already he felt he'd been led on a greased-pig chase. They had followed the stream, picking up just enough sign of tracks to know Slattery's horse was being kept in the water. An hour after they'd left Gann's, Whaleen had looked north and had spotted a wagon far out on the prairie, only a dot on the horizon, but heading straight for Rock Spring. That's all they had seen. Now Vreeland sat without a movement, staring in a wide sweep from south around to east. The big stretch of country was brown with burned grass. The midafternoon sun was driving hot on him and his stallion. Easily, he nudged the horse off the bank into the coolness of the water and shade thrown by the trees.

"What do you think, Dan?" asked Paul Lutz. "He rode near enough to the rest of his gang long enough to let them know we'd be comin'? Then he led us on this chase?"

"He's smart," said Whaleen. His boney, square-jawed features were drawn out and tired, his white shirt glued with sticky sweat to his shoulders. "Too damn smart."

"Those tracks go east," Vreeland told them. "That ransom isn't due to be paid 'til late tonight. We still have time."

"Unless the plan for payment has been changed," Lutz offered. He watched Vreeland casually, made the statement something which had simply run through his mind. "You'd want to be in there."

Vreeland gave no answer. He eased forward to stand in the stirrups, relaxed his tired legs and body. The stallion lifted its head to shake the drops of wetness from its face. Vreeland rubbed the horse's long thick neck, kneading his fingers deep into the smooth hair, relaxing the corded muscles under the leathery skin. He pulled the reins gently to the left.

"Let them make their own time," he said to Lutz and Whaleen. "If we spot Slattery, spread the target."

An hour later they struck the wagon road

which paralleled the railroad north for two miles and then turned east directly into Rock Spring. The sod was indented in three distinct spots by wheel tracks. At least five or six horses had come by today. Slattery's mount's hoofprints were lost among the others.

"He's smart," Lutz said, agreeing with Rube Whaleen. "We could ride all week and not pick up a clear trail again."

Vreeland dismounted and stood in the roadway while he studied the hardpack. To the west the sun had lost some of its harsh glare of day, but its heat still plastered his shirt and Levi's to his backside. Slattery could've either gone east or west. The one thing Vreeland regretted was that he had partially believed what Slattery had said in the hotel. The man had seemed so outright sincere . . . He'd even let him keep the filed-down Navy Colt he'd had under his belt.

Vreeland stared west, watched for a minute the sharp yellow of the sun gradually changing along the prairie to glow in vivid hues of gold and orange. No sense in going back to Gann's. Even if Slattery had cut around by there again, Milo and his wife were in town.

"We'll go back and wait for them to collect that money," he said. "Slattery'll be in on that. He won't ride clear of town. I can promise you that."

Patricia Hughes stared at Slattery. "My parents believed it would broaden me to make the trip," she said. "I was never good at talking and they thought a great deal of travel would give me something to talk about."

"They were just trying to help you."

She smiled. "I know. But I tried to explain ... It isn't that I can't feel easy with people." Her smile turned into low laughter. "There are some people it's easy to talk to. I felt that about you when I saw you on the train."

Slattery looked toward the doorway at the same time as the woman. Fox stood there, attracted by the sound of her laughter. His whiskered face was dark in the lamplight, but neither of them missed the way his eyes moved from the neckline of Patricia's dress, down across her bosom to her stomach and the lines of her legs beneath her dress.

"You think somethin's funny," he said, smiling at her. "I'll show you how funny things are."

Flora Gann appeared in the doorway beside the tall gunman. From behind them Joe Paxton said, "Okay, Al. They're not goin' anywhere."

The smirk broadened on Fox's face. "She's goin' though. Soon as that dirt eater gets

110

back." He nodded knowingly at Patricia. "I didn't think you had spirit. I like spirit."

"Al," called Joe Paxton. "Baine's raised fifty. It's to you."

The tall gunman left the doorway and Flora Gann said to Patricia and Slattery, "You haven't had a drink all day. Would you like water?"

"No water," Fox snapped at her. "She wants water she c'n ask for it." He laughed and Allerby and Baine guffawed with him. "Get away from there, you."

Flora Gann left the doorway. Patricia's eyes didn't shift from the other room, yet despite the inference in Fox's words she seemed calmer, more controlled. She said softly to Slattery, "You can act fast and have the roof open. They'll be so busy with their card game, they'll take a minute to get up. If I'm in the doorway."

"Anyone of them would shoot you to get past." He listened with her to the rough talk and obscene cursing that had gone on all afternoon, realizing it must be close to sunset. Gann would return soon and Paxton would take the girl. What could happen on the ride into town could be far worse than being held like this. She wasn't the withdrawn, weak person he'd thought inside the train coach, but she had a strength and a warmth she

111

kept hidden within herself. They had talked all afternoon, the girl telling him about her life in Boston, he giving her a completely different picture of life on a Texas ranch as a boy, and how after his mother had died in the bad winter of sixty-eight he, his brother and father had ridden north to Kansas to stake out land. The violence of the fight against the land grabbers in which his father and brother had been killed, what the South was really like after the war between the States, had appalled her, and he'd seen tears in her eyes. Her life had been so different. She'd been so young she remembered mainly the absence of her father and how she'd grown up so close to her mother because of the war.

He could see her as a girl, self-conscious, somehow always afraid of saying the wrong thing, or in speaking out of turn and sounding silly. "You blamed yourself," he had said, "for being on the train. Your parents made the decision to visit Mexico. This isn't all your fault."

"The trip was for me, so I'd change," she'd said.

"You're talking now," he had told her. And she'd smiled for the first time.

She smiled in a different way now, as she straightened on the bed and stood. "They won't shoot me," she said in a low, sure voice.

112

"Get ready. You can be outside and running toward the barn. It's your only chance."

Slattery was clear of the chair, his hand reaching out to stop her. "Hear that," he said. "I wouldn't get through the hole."

The drumming of a horse's hoofs and rumble of a wagon came past the rear of the soddy and slowed toward the front door. Patricia Hughes halted near the doorway.

"Gann would shoot me before I could pull myself up," Slattery said. "Wait."

He was beside her, not touching her, yet ready to grip and hold her arm. A draft of warm evening air with the smell of dried grass to it came into the soddy with Gann, then died as the door closed behind him.

Gann broke into speech the moment he reached the table. "Hughes has sent for the money," he told everyone, his voice high and excited. "A message came through from Fort Worth they'd rush it in by eight tonight."

"The whole hundred-thousand?" asked Fox.

"Every last greenback of it. They're rushin' the railroad section crew so a train can bring it. They've backed the train the girl came in on west so the station'll be clear. Hughes has asked that everybody keep clear of the station 'cept Lutz."

Allerby howled in a loud, happy laugh.

113

"Dammit, everythin' we wanted. Every last thing. It'll go right, Joe. It can't miss goin' right."

"We'll move soon as it's dark enough," Paxton told the men crowded around the table. "Baine, you'll ride straight in and get the full directions to Hughes on how we want the money delivered."

Milo Gann said, "Joe, I stopped at the station. I didn't see Lutz. I thought he told us to be sure . . ."

"Shut! Shut up!" Joe Paxton snapped. The dirt floor was scuffed, a chair went skidding back against the wall, and Paxton loomed up in the doorway five short feet's distance from Slattery and the girl.

"You heard," the gunman said. He shook his head. Paxton scowled. "I was sure about you, Slattery, but not about her. Now I got no choice."

"You have with her," Slattery said. "She won't say a word. You can have Lutz get out of town with you."

"No, we can't," Al Fox said, stepping in alongside Paxton. He stood slouched over a bit, hip-cocked, his thumbs in his crossed belts, his eyes on the bosom of the girl's dress. "Lutz stays in town. He likes the town."

Slattery edged in front of the girl. "How

many will this count up to?" he asked Fox. "With both of us?"

"Huh?" Fox straightened, his hands didn't move.

Slattery nodded at the double gun rig. "You must cut notches or something. How deep do you cut for a woman. Or a man you get in the back?"

Fox cursed softly, swept his right hand along his side to the revolver butt.

"Please! Please don't," Flora Gann said. "Not in here! Please, you don't have to kill them!"

Joe Paxton slapped Fox's hand down. "Not now. We don't know who's out there. You hold!"

"I do it my own way," Fox snarled, his stare burned into Slattery. "I'll catch up. I do it like I want, Joe."

"Yes. Just hold down now."

Fox's stare didn't change. "I'll promise you this, mouth," he said to Slattery. "You'll see it comin', I promise you'll know exactly how you're gettin' it."

Chapter Twelve

Fox backed from the doorway with Paxton, who motioned for Flora Gann to precede them to the table. Talk went on, but it was held down so Slattery and the girl couldn't hear. Slattery realized how quiet the bedroom had become. He turned and looked at Patricia Hughes. She was sitting on the bed, her knees drawn up to her chin, staring at the dirt floor with a dazed, lost expression.

Slattery moved past her and sat down beside her. "Patricia, the last thing you should do is give up."

"You shouldn't have come out here. You should have let them keep me."

"You know better than that."

She stared up at Slattery pleadingly. "Fox won't leave here until you're dead. He wants that more than reward money."

"You had nothing to do with that."

"I did. You wouldn't be here if it weren't for me."

He looked at her closely, her mouth shaking at the corners to keep from crying. "Fox would have come after me sooner or later. Once he found out I shot his cousin."

Her eyes closed and she shook her head, not accepting the statement. She spoke very calmly, very quietly. "I've thought and thought about what they'd do to me. I could identify every one of them, and they know it. The way I've been all my life, I tried to tell myself it didn't matter." Her eyes opened, raised to his. "But it does matter. There ought to be a special penalty they should pay for what kidnapping does to a person. It's more than murder." She paused. "I know what'll happen to me, and all I want is for you to get away. It shouldn't have to happen to you, too."

"Get hold of yourself, Patricia."

She shook her head slowly, wearily. "I do have control of myself. I just can't stop realizing I've caused this. Even before we'd left Boston, I caused it. Poor Maria Perani. I caused that, too."

Slattery was silent a full minute, watching her. The smell of wood smoke was strong in the room. Gann's wife was getting the evening meal. They were so sure of themselves, with their low talk, and having their food before they started out. He said to Patricia, "Get through feeling sorry for yourself, and we'll try to think of some way to work out of this."

She stared at him, more surprised at the snap in his voice than hurt.

"Listen," Slattery said. "I came out here as much to clear my name as I did to help you. You know that. You can go on blaming yourself for everything, and you can sit right here until they finish in there and take us out. Or you can help me plan something that will save both of us. I'll tell you this. We both have to stand up and work if we're going to come out of this alive."

"But I can't help," Patricia moaned. She glanced toward the smell of the fire and frying steak, brushed her lips with the round of her hand. "I can't do anything."

"You're not sure whether you can or can't. We've got to keep our eyes open and watch."

Seeing her head begin to shake again, he gripped her shoulders. "These men intend to kill me. They intend to kill you. Mine'll come easy, but it won't be as fast and easy for you. Not once Fox gets to you." He stood and moved to the doorway.

Gann and Baine sat with their backs to the bedroom. Paxton and Fox faced his way and could see the shifting of a shadow on the wall if he tried to stand on the bed. He mulled over the idea to douse the lamp and shove the boards off the roof. Then he dropped that. The boards might stick long enough for a gun to be fired. Bullets would be aimed directly at the bed. He could have Patricia half-way, two-thirds outside, but she'd still be hit.

He stepped as carefully backwards as he'd gone to the door. Patricia had gotten up from the bed. "I'm sorry for acting like that." She hesitated. "I just felt . . ."

"I know how you felt. You have no reason to though. Not here, or when you were on the train. Or before you left Boston."

She stared at him, not fully comprehending his reasoning.

He said, "You think no man wants you because you're quiet and you don't know what to say."

"I told you that because I believed you'd understand," she said obstinately. She looked away from him.

"Look, you're as much of a woman as any I've seen. You've watched how Fox doesn't take his eyes off you. You're more woman than you realize, and it's about time you woke up to it!"

"It isn't the same with a man like Fox."

"Don't give me that 'it isn't the same' talk. It is the same, if you make it be. All you've done is sit quiet and cute and wait for something to happen. You have to do something on your own, whether it's getting away or being a woman!"

Her eyes were looking into his, bright and wet, as though she would cry. Suddenly, her

119

arms raised and circled his shoulders and she kissed him, holding him to her tight and hard until he felt her whole body relax against his.

He held her as tightly, his mouth close to her ear. He said, "We'll get out of this. You do what I say when the chance comes, and we'll both get out of this alive." Her hair brushed his mouth as she nodded.

"Well, damn me," Al Fox said. He stood in the bedroom doorway, chuckled softly to himself, watched the girl drop her arms from around Slattery's shoulders. He wore his flat-crowned black hat pushed high onto his forehead, and he chewed absently on the drawstring. "Glad to see the little lady's got life." The chuckle became obscene. "Damn me if I ain't glad."

"What you waitin' for, Al?" said Joe Paxton from the table.

Slattery did not let go of the girl. "When I move you run. Get to the river and keep in the trees."

Patricia Hughes gave no sign Slattery had spoken. She kept looking at Fox as she had when he'd first spoken.

"Move," Fox ordered. The thumbs hooked into his double gun rig lowered threateningly. "You want it right here, Slattery."

"No, not in my house," Flora Gann said.

"Mr. Paxton, you promised there wouldn't be any killing."

"Shut up!" her husband told the woman.

"But we didn't know . . ."

"Shut up! Just shut up!"

Slattery nudged Patricia's arm and started her toward the doorway. He said nothing more, kept his attention on Fox, not positive what the gunman would do. If he intended to shoot now, there wasn't a chance.

Fox backed from the doorway. Patricia went through ahead of Slattery. Baine and Allerby hadn't finished eating. Paxton was at the outside door with Milo Gann. Gann was not armed, from what Slattery could see.

"Lead the wagon in close," Paxton was saying to Gann. "Look around first, just in case."

"Ain't no danger anyone followed me," Gann gold him. "I circled wide north so's I wouldn't bump into Dan Vreeland."

"It's not only your tracks," Paxton said. "They could've picked up the palomino's trail."

"No chance of that," offered Baine. "I kept on the road 'til I hit the creek, Joe. I stayed in the channel all the way here."

"Check anyway," Paxton ordered emphatically. He pulled open the door.

The instant the big homesteader was outside, he shut it and stepped to the table.

"Hold it there," he told Slattery. And, nodding to Fox, "Ride him good and clear of the creek. When he's found I don't want anyone tyin' him to this place."

"He'll be good and far," Fox said. He nudged Slattery ahead, eyed Patricia Hughes. He grinned . . . "I'll catch up with you plenty of time 'fore she goes to the station."

Patricia walked slowly toward the door, showing how tired and worn she was after a full day without food. Outside the ranch wagon creaked and the horse snorted while Gann backed them close to the soddy. Slattery moved as slowly as the girl, his shoulders slouched to seem as tired, his face blank, like he'd given up hope. But his eyes were alive, took in the Navy Colt still on the mantlepiece, and the muzzle-loading long rifle. He couldn't be certain the rifle was loaded, or that they hadn't emptied the Colt's cylinder. He edged to the left, watched the men, and Patricia, almost at the door.

Paxton stepped past him, went directly to the fireplace and took the Navy Colt. "They'd only need to find this in here," he said. He jammed the weapon down beneath his huge silver buckles. He had halted exactly between Slattery and the rifle. "Right to the door, behind her," the gunman directed, both hands on his own guns. "She gets in the wagon. You and Fox'll go to the barn."

Baine was on his feet at the door. The wagon noises had ceased outside. Baine gripped the latch to pull the door inward and allow Patricia to pass.

With Paxton and Allerby beyond the table and Fox behind him, Slattery got ready. Gann didn't have a gun outside. He could block Baine at the door, and the rest would be held back a few precious seconds. The fact that Paxton didn't want any shooting now was his main hope. The door was opening . . .

"Now! Go! Run!" he screamed to Patricia. He jumped, dived at Baine, striking the shocked gunman square in the chest with both outstretched hands, shoving him back.

Patricia was in the doorway, through. Slattery, erect on his feet, still moved in a fast turn to follow her outside.

Milo Gann was like a stone wall, his immense form blocking the girl even before she reached the level of the ground. Above them the wagon and horses were thick black shadows closing out the moonlight. Gann grunted while one huge arm shot out to grasp Slattery.

Slattery heard Patricia's, "No, Tom!" as he swung around to face Paxton, Fox and

123

Allerby, all closing in with drawn six-guns.

Life hung in the instant silence.

Paxton gestured wildly with his revolver. "Don't shoot! Don't!" He calmed with the spoken words, snapped at Gann. "Take her! Tie her feet and hands and throw the canvas over here in the wagon!" He leveled his weapon at Slattery, "Al, get him out of here. Watch him!"

Fox slashed down with the steel barrel of the gun in his right hand, caught Slattery flush along the collarbone. Sharp pain drove into Slattery's shoulder, cut into his chest and neck as he was shoved bodily outside.

Staggering to regain his feet, Slattery felt Fox grab his left arm, then throw him in the direction of the barn.

"Keep goin'." Fox's voice, low and cold, snarled the order. "I don't give a damn about Gann. I'll kill you right here!"

Slattery caught himself before he fell, kept his body erect. As Fox shoved him again, he thought he heard Patricia cry out in pain. But all sound was lost under the rumble and rattle the wagon made when it started to roll.

Chapter Thirteen

At the barn door Fox dropped a stride behind Slattery. "Open the door," the gunman directed, "so I can see you."

Slattery pulled at the heavy wood, felt the shoulder that had been slammed throb. A lighted lamp hung above the center of the long, wide aisle. The four stalls on the right were empty. A buggy, badly in need of repair, was backed into the open space beyond them. The palomino and a long-legged grey gelding waited in the two rear left stalls. Slattery halted before he reached the thick shadows between the animals.

"Saddle them," Fox said. He holstered one of his six-guns. He gestured at his own horse when he slid his Henry rifle from its sheath. "Mine, then yours."

Slattery reached up and took Fox's saddle down from the two-by-four that separated the stalls. While he worked, he glanced about the building. The back door was a good twenty feet away, with the ladder to the hay mow the only cover in that direction. No chance to move toward the front of the barn. Fox had spotted himself directly opposite the palomino. Slattery couldn't run five feet before the cocked Colt would cut him down.

Slattery finished with the gelding's cinch, habitually pulled at the strap to check it. "Out here," Fox said. "Do yours in the aisle."

Fox had holstered his other revolver. He climbed into the saddle, sat easily during the time it took to lead out the palomino. He leaned forward a bit, the Henry's muzzle pointed directly at Slattery's head. He did not say a word until Slattery had mounted and reined the palomino toward the front door.

"Through the back," Fox said. "Straight to the creek and then stick to the channel. You go 'head and try somethin'. I don't give one single damn 'bout Gann or his wife."

Slattery did exactly as he was told. The moon was high, almost full, so bright he could see Flora Gann standing near the doorway of her home watching them leave.

Fox kept two good horses' lengths behind him, his Henry rested across the pommel. Paxton had said a mile along the river, Slattery thought, and as far into the prairie on the opposite bank. Gann's wagon must be two miles away. Going into the dark line of brush, Slattery glanced northeast, his eyes resting for a moment on the barn roof glistening in the moonlight. The long

126

building stood like a silent sentry guarding the spacious emptiness of the prairie that rose and went down and rose again until the starshine cut the horizon. Only the rustle of the slight river breeze through the cottonwoods' leaves broke the peace of the landscape, the absence of sound, accenting the irony of what was happening, masking the hate and intent of the gunman. Slattery tightened his fingers on the thin strip of leather and turned the palomino into the water.

The splash and pull of the horse's hoofs was louder than the ripple of the current over the sandbars and rocks.

"Hold it down," Fox warned. He kneed his grey, jabbed Slattery's spine with the muzzle.

Slattery slowed his horse nd Fox dropped back.

Slattery half-turned his face, tried to watch Fox's movements, to wait for the gunman to glance aside. Fox said, "The back of your head's all I want to see. Keep it like that."

Slattery rode on. He held the palomino as quiet as possible, not able to look for an opportunity to act.

They rode in silence for another quarter-mile before Fox again pulled up close and jabbed the barrel into Slattery's back. "Over to the right bank," the gunman ordered. "Stay at the edge." Fox dropped behind, rigidly kept the two horses' lengths distance.

Slattery obeyed, but with hope now. Twice Fox had moved in near him to give directions. A warm tightness coursed through Slattery's body. Fox would have to tell him when to climb the bank. He calmed the feeling of hope, waited . . .

A hundred yards ahead the trees broke off into a small moonlit grass-covered park. The area was clearly defined, almost daylight bright, and Slattery knew Fox wouldn't let them get into the open. He waited, watched for the gunman to pull up.

But Fox didn't move in close. "Onto the bank," he said in a loud voice. "Slow."

Slattery's heart started to pound. The warmth began to drain out of him. A stand of willows, spotted by a few cottonwoods, was all that separated them from the flat. Fox could fall further and further behind and still have a clean target once they were under the floodlight glare of the moon. Slattery kneed the palomino hard and the horse kicked and splashed to climb the high bank.

"Slow. Hold it down." Fox snapped. He spurred his grey, came closer, the Henry's barrel held out to jab like a bayonet into Slattery's ribs.

Slattery's pulse raced, then stood still as he felt the steel muzzle strike. He whirled around in the saddle, shoved away the barrel, jabbing his spurs into the palomino so the animal's flank slammed the grey's side.

The rifle banged, sending the bullet harmlessly across the flat. Thrown against the pommel. Fox swore wildly, grabbed for the horn to hold the saddle. In the few seconds it took him to turn his horse, Slattery plunged the palomino down the bank into the creek.

Slattery lay forward across the pommel, his chest and shoulders pressed to the horse's thick neck. The palomino climbed the bank, pushed into brush, running as hard as he could, but Slattery realized it wasn't fast enough. He kicked the animal, drove him onto the top of the bank, knowing his freedom was only temporary once the stronger long-legged grey crossed the streambed.

The rifle cracked once, and again, zinging bullets inches above his head. One slug whapped solidly into a cottonwood trunk, the second sang in a high whine onto the flat.

The palomino was through the timber, galloping at the edge of the open moonlit prairie. The muscles of its neck were tight and strained under Slattery's cheek. Water splashed loudly behind them, and Slattery pulled the horse to the left.

He slowed the animal, let it go down the

bank and into the water at its own pace. Once on the opposite bank, Slattery broke through to the flat and dug his spurs into the sweating flanks.

The shift had thrown Fox off long enough to get the lead he needed. Slattery leaned back in the saddle, took his weight from the bobbing neck, let the horse slow and get its wind ... He'd made a half-mile, then another quarter before the Henry banged twice far behind him.

Slattery crossed the river once more, spurred the palomino through the brush. Five hundred yards to his left, Gann's barn was a black silver-roofed silhouette in the moonlight.

He rode another minute, then reined in. He couldn't hear Fox's horse, but the gunman would be in the open before the palomino reached the soddy. Slattery swung down. He turned the blowing animal into the brush, slapped its sweat-drenched flank, drove it back into the water. Crouching low, he kept to the brush and headed for the soddy.

He heard the palomino splash through the channel. Hoofs pounded the ground behind him while Fox came ahead noisily. Slattery stopped, hidden by the brush, watched the horse and rider go into the trees.

Slattery straightened and ran for Gann's

homestead. He wasn't certain the muzzle-loader was fit to fire, or if it had been left inside the soddy, but it was the only weapon he could get.

The barn was four long-legged strides ahead when Fox's yell came from the river, followed immediately by a shot.

Slattery bent low, heard the bee-buzz of the lead slug go past. Another shot cracked, another, both bullets kicking up small bomb-bursts of dirt ahead of him. The grey's hoofs thumped loudly, closed in on him.

Flora Gann was in the doorway of the soddy, etched in the yellowish square of lamplight. She stared out into the night long enough to see Slattery running toward her, and Fox crossing the flat beyond the barn.

The woman ducked back into the room, grabbed at the doorlatch to pull it shut. Slattery reached the closing door. He got hold of the edge and yanked it open. He dashed inside, past the terrified woman, to the fireplace.

The long rifle lay against the stones. He had it in his hands, checked it, and it was loaded.

Fox's grey had reached the barn, came toward the soddy at a full gallop. The single shot would be no match for Fox's two six-guns.

"Into the bedroom," Slattery told Flora Gann.

The woman was terrified, nailed where she stood, listening to the horse outside, her eyes riveted on the rifle in Slattery's hands.

"Behind the fireplace," said Slattery. He motioned at the stones while he backed into the bedroom. "Quick, he'll shoot through the doors."

Three steps and he was at the bed. He stepped up, felt the boards under the mattress sink with his weight. He pushed with the palm of his hand on the ceiling hole. The thin wood gave and lifted. Sand poured from the rooftop onto Slattery's head and shoulders while he pulled himself up.

Fox's horse was stopping, the tall gunman swinging clear of the saddle at the soddy door. The instant his boots touched dirt, Fox had both Colts coming out of their holsters.

Slattery was on the roof, balanced on one knee, leveling the rifle.

Fox aimed his guns as swiftly as he took his stride. Both weapons spat flame. Slattery felt one bullet tug at his coat sleeve, the other burn the hair and flesh above his right ear as he fired.

Fox slowed in mid-stride, staggered. The expression on his face was lost beneath the brim of his hat. He swayed and pitched forward.

Slattery charged off the roof, the blood from his wound spreading along the hairline and over his ear. The rifle barrel held above his head like a club, he jumped down onto Fox.

Fox didn't move. Slattery kicked the Colt out of the gunman's right hand, pulled the weapon from the left. He rolled the body onto its back. The large stain of blood that spread visibly through the shirt above the heart glinted darkly in the moonlight.

Slattery dropped the rifle and picked up the second six-gun. His head lowered, he broke the weapon and emptied the six cartridges into his hand, then shoved them into his pants pocket. Straightening, he dropped the empty gun, jammed the other under his belt. He wiped the wetness from his ear with his coat sleeve.

Flora Gann opened the soddy door. Slattery, taking hold of the grey's bridle, turned the horse so he could mount.

"You're bleeding," Flora Gann said. "I have some cloth inside."

"Haven't got time," said Slattery. He placed his foot in the stirrup, began to swing up.

"You're bleeding too bad. You won't . . ." Flora Gann stopped her

133

talk. She shivered involuntarily, not from the slight night chill, but from what she'd suddenly seen on Slattery's face.

"Don't hurt my husband," she pleaded. "He only wanted the barn. Please." She stepped alongside the horse, ran a few strides as Slattery spurred the animal. "Please, I tried to feed you! I did! I tried to help! Don't hurt my husband!"

Chapter Fourteen

Peter Walkens was busy restocking his shelves and counters when the rock was thrown.

The day had been a busy one. After everything that had happened since last night, it seemed each citizen of Rock Spring, and those who'd heard of the kidnapping at the ranches throughout the county, had come in today. The general store had been the one place they'd all visited. Most would have eventually, anyway, now it was near the end of the summer when they came in to buy school things for their kids and to stock up for the winter. Just the same, today there had been more than usual, each one talking and wanting to know every fact about what had happened. Where was the girl now? How was the ransom going to be paid! What had Dan Vreeland done about it, anyway? They'd stood on the store porch and steps and had tried to get a look at the Hughes man and woman. But both of the girl's parents had stayed in their hotel room. Walkens had finished pricing some blue work shirts. He'd glanced satisfied, contentedly about the long wide room as he walked up the middle aisle past counters and shelves and racks that bulged with pants and coats, fresh bolts of dry goods, bright prints and percales and calicoes, underwear, bandannas, the gun rack and hardware, all the products which spoke of his thriving business. He'd stopped at the candy case to put out more peppermint sticks, when his big front window crashed in.

Walkens dropped the candy box. The thin red and white peppermint sticks rolled on the floor. Hiram Chadwick, who'd been working in the rear storeroom, ran past the huge iron coffee grinder.

Walkens was at the window, bending to pick up the rock. He watched the shattered glass, fearful another stone might come through.

"What happened?" Chadwick asked. When he saw the rock, and the paper tied around it, his mouth dropped open.

Walkens had the string untied, read the note. "Get the sheriff," he said. "And tell those people at the Sorento it's for them."

Chadwick turned the key in the door, opened it, and bumped into Dan Vreeland. The sheriff had his six-gun in his hand. He holstered the revolver, stepped inside. He left the door open for those who crossed Boulder behind him to look and listen.

Walkens held out the note. "It tells how the ransom's to be paid, Dan." His gaze flicked to the window. "Why my store? I have nothin' to do with any of it."

Vreeland scanned the note, inked in large stark black letters.

HAVE MONEY TAKEN FROM TRAIN IN BAG TO RR STATION. STATION AGENT COUNTS MONEY TO MAKE SURE 100,000 IN TEN PACKS. MOVE TRAINS FROM STATION. AGENT BRINGS MONEY OUT TO CORRAL AT EIGHT O'CLOCK. GIRL LET FREE AFTER BAG IS HOOKED ON FAR CORRAL POST.

Outside, the chatter went on, the voices confused. "I was just leaving the Drovers," one man said. "I was locking up my store," said another. I was doing this; I was doing

136

that. All quieted when the sheriff asked, "Did anyone see who threw the rock?"

No one answered.

Sheriff Vreeland gestured at the street. "The one who threw it had to be out front. Someone must have seen him. Was he alone?" Still only silence. "All right, break up. Get back to your homes."

"Is it about the ransom, Dan?" a man called. "Can we help."

"You'll help most by goin' home and keepin' your families inside. Go ahead now." Vreeland started past the crowd. His tall, heavy-set deputy was breaking a path through the onlookers. "Jack," Vreeland called over the heads and hats. "Find Paul Lutz. Get him into the hotel."

Peter Walkens touched the lawman's arm. "What about my window? It cost eighty dollars all the way from Dallas."

Vreeland jerked his arm from the store owner's hand and walked onto the porch. Walkens' voice carried through the night to him as he crossed the alleyway and onto the Sorento House steps. A girl's life depended on this note, and the storekeeper could only cry about his window ... Vreeland glanced up and down Boulder. The entire length of the street was almost daylight bright under the moon and stars. The flat would be as clear,

137

clearer at eight o'clock, with the moon higher overhead than it was this early. There wasn't a chance of circling the area with men to close in on the ones who had the girl. Not if they were going to get her back alive.

William Hughes and his wife were at the bottom of the staircase with Hiram Chadwick. Ugo Perani had come out of the kitchen.

William Hughes' thin face wrinkled like an old man's while he read the inked words. His wife seemed calmer, more composed. "We'll do exactly as they want, Sheriff," she said. "Exactly."

"You can't be sure they'll let your daughter go," Vreeland told them. "This isn't what I wanted, Mrs. Hughes."

"This is what the men who have her want," William Hughes said. "This is what we want."

Vreeland said, "The best way is to make them come close to the town. Once they have the money, we'd be sure to get the girl. You should handle the money yourself. You do it like this . . ."

"We'll do what they ask," said Hughes emotionally. "I don't care about the money. Just as long as the exchange is made."

"Mr. Hughes," said Vreeland, "we're not certain Lutz will agree to this. He'd be puttin' himself in a tough spot."

"Then I'll do it myself, if he won't do it," Hughes told him. "They won't know the difference."

Edna Hughes said, "They will know. The station man is tall and husky. He's easy to watch at night. He'd be alone at the station. That's why they chose him."

The porch screen door swished inward and Paul Lutz entered the lobby with the deputy. Kennedy immediately halted and held the door shut so the townspeople couldn't crowd in. Lutz wore his visored cap and black dust cuffs on his sleeves. He had come directly from the telegraph desk. He stared questioningly at the lawman, then at Mr. and Mrs. Hughes.

"The money will be here by eight," he told them. "The company is sending only an engine so it will travel faster."

William Hughes handed the station agent the ransom note. "Are you willing to do this, Mr. Lutz?"

Lutz's mouth moved slightly while he formed the words, reading the note hastily the first time. He read the paper again, rubbed his jaw worriedly, unsure of himself.

He looked at William and Edna Hughes. "I'm not sure. I'd be out there all alone." His gaze shifted to Vreeland.

"That's right," the sheriff told him.

"They'll be at least out past the corral. Maybe further."

"You do this, I'll make it worth..." William Hughes began.

"I'd do it because I wanted to help," said Paul Lutz. "But I'd be all alone." He kept his eyes on Vreeland for verification.

"Mr. and Mrs. Hughes want it that way," the lawman said. "I'll have men ready and waiting the minute you're back with the girl, but you'd be all alone."

"He has to be alone," William Hughes said. "Sheriff, you can't have men ready to chase them. One of them could be watching the street now. They're too clever not to know what you're doing. That fight was planned so carefully, and their tearing up the railroad. This note was thrown through the window by someone who was right here in Rock Spring. You can't have anyone ready. Please, clear the streets and make the people stay in their houses."

Vreeland looked from Lutz to the Hughes'. "You can't expect a man to go out alone. It's too dangerous."

"Sheriff," said Paul Lutz. "I know I'll be taking a chance, but Mr. Hughes is right." His stare rested on the husband and wife, his smooth tanned features showing complete sympathy for them. "I'll be able to bring their

140

daughter back only if the kidnappers know I'm not in on any trick."

"You'll do it, then," Edna Hughes breathed. "Oh, thank you. Thank you."

Paul Lutz said, "I'll do exactly what the note says, Mrs. Hughes." He turned to Vreeland. "Sheriff, I think both of the trains should be moved, so they'll be able to see I'm alone."

Nodding, Vreeland spoke to William and Edna Hughes. "You better wait here. We'll bring your daughter straight to you." He slipped his watch from his vest pocket, nodded to the fat hotel owner as he turned. "Seven-twenty now. Ugo, I'll depend on you."

The hotelman nodded, remained alongside the girl's parents. William Hughes said as Paul Lutz started to leave with the lawman, "I know you don't want money, Mr. Lutz, but ... I'll see you afterward. I will." He took hold of his wife's arm. She was more confident than she had been, yet she was close to breaking down.

Vreeland said to the deputy at the door, "Move the people off the streets, Jack. Every man, woman and kid is to stay inside until we have the girl. Make sure."

"I will, Dan." The deputy pushed the screen door open, held it for Vreeland to follow onto the porch. Paul Lutz was beside the lawman, his face lowered to Vreeland's.

"I don't have a gun, Dan," whispered Lutz. "You have a small derringer I could slip into my pocket. They wouldn't know. I'd have a better chance if something went wrong."

"I've got one," said Vreeland. "Come over to the office and I'll give it to you."

Tom Slattery kept his body low while he edged alongside the flatcar at the rear of the train. He'd noted that the train had been backed from the station when he was still a quarter-mile out on the prairie. He had tied Fox's grey horse behind the small shed where Ugo Perani had waited with the palomino. Now, he could see the station office was empty. No one or nothing moved on the platform. Slattery halted, then retraced his steps to the flatcar. He couldn't wait for Paul Lutz to appear. That might take too long. He did not know which house belonged to Lutz, but he knew the man to ask.

He circled wide around the residential district, kept to the shadows. The homes were different tonight. When he'd left Rock Spring, although it was early morning, house windows were open to catch the night coolness. The windows he passed now were locked tight and not a sound came from the homes. Slattery trotted along the side of the last house and stopped near the front porch. The New England type park was empty and silent. Except for three horses tied at the Drovers Bar hitchrail, Boulder was deserted. The thick blackness of the church steeple looked higher than it was. Beyond it the top floor of the two-story hotel blended with the steeple into a wall of darkness. From far to the north he heard the low, prolonged blast of a train whistle. The sound faded off and died in the intense quiet.

Slattery could smell chicken frying before he reached the yard behind the Sorento House. He was fully aware of the emptiness in his stomach while he carefully moved to the kitchen window. If he was this tired from hunger after just one day, then Patricia Hughes must be far worse.

Ugo Perani was in the kitchen, his broad back to the window as he prepared the chicken and stirred something in a small kettle. Slattery tapped on the glass.

The hotelman looked toward the closed dining room door. When Slattery tapped again, Ugo gazed through the window. Sudden fear came into the round, mustached face. Hurriedly, Ugo unlocked the rear door.

"You can't take a chance on..." the hotelman began. His hand rose to touch the side of Slattery's head. "That is bad, Thomas. You've lost so much blood."

"How's Maria, Ugo?"

"Better. Much better. She woke this morning and talked. She's sleeping now." His face was grim, concerned. "I'll heat water, Thomas, and clean the wound."

Slattery shook his head. A sharp pain shot along his ear into the tendons of his head. Feeling had become dulled during his long ride, but with a toss of his head the wound throbbed in a slow, steady rhythm. "Which house does Paul Lutz own? I want him."

"Paul Lutz? He's helping . . ."

"He's the man who set up the kidnapping."

Ugo was shocked. "No. He couldn't, Thomas. He is helping Mr. and Mrs. Hughes." He told Slattery about the note that had been thrown through the general store window. "Paul agreed to help get the girl back."

"Which house is his, Ugo?"

Slowly, Ugo Perani's head shook. "I believe you were not part of what happened. But I cannot believe Paul is either." He didn't finish what he intended to say. Maria had called his name from the bedroom, and Ugo answered. "Yes, I'm coming." He watched Slattery. "I'll be right out. Let me clean that wound. I have chicken and soup on the stove." He turned

144

toward the bedroom, hadn't taken a step when the dining room door swung inward.

Sheriff Vreeland came in. His small slender face tightened, his black eyes sharp and hard at seeing Slattery. His right hand swept back and down, flicked open the holster flap. Slattery didn't make a move. Ugo swung away from the bedroom door, threw up his hands as the lawman drew his .45.

"Don't! Don't!" he cried. "Don't kill him, Sheriff! Don't!"

Chapter Fifteen

Vreeland's thumb snapped back the hammer. He said, "Open your coat, Slattery. Slow."

Slattery's hands remained at his sides. "You're wrong, Sheriff. I'm not in on the kidnapping." In the small silence, Maria Perani called, "Ugo, Ugo!", then said something in Italian. Her husband hesitated, flustered, fearful of what would happen. "Give him your gun, Thomas. He could have shot you."

"Shootin's too easy for you," Vreeland said to Slattery. "I want to see you swing for what you've done to these people." The muzzle

145

inched upward, directly into Slattery's face. He stepped forward to take Slattery's six-gun.

"Sheriff, the train's coming in," said Slattery. "Paul Lutz is the man you want. He planned the kidnapping." He backstepped, preventing the lawman from touching his coatfront. "I've got proof, Sheriff. You stopped at Gann's soddy today. You didn't know it, but you had guns aimed at your front and your back. You remember how Lutz kept his horse a little behind yours?"

"You were inside?" Vreeland said. "You made the Ganns..." Maria Perani called once more and Vreeland nodded to the hotelman. "Go ahead, Ugo." Then, again to Slattery, "If you had somethin' on Lutz why didn't you take him?"

"I was being held myself." The lawman paused, kept the revolver leveled but he made no motion to touch Slattery while Slattery told him how he and Patricia Hughes were kept in the soddy. Ugo came out of the bedroom when Slattery was finishing with, "You think about it, Sheriff. That note should've had either you or the girl's father take the money out to them. With Lutz holding the money, he has his way out of town."

Ugo Perani said, "Thomas, Paul Lutz has lived in our town five years. Why would he wait until now to do this?"

146

"He didn't have a wealthy family coming through before." He looked at Vreeland. "Lutz knew the Hughes family would be on the train. He knew when they left Mexico City. He had plenty of time to get Paxton's gang and to bribe the Gann's. You saw Gann's new barn. How would he pay for that?"

Vreeland had listened thoughtfully. He was doubtful. Yet he still hadn't moved closer to Slattery. The train whistle wailed in the night outside, less than a mile's distance from Rock Spring. Slattery said, "Sheriff, I'll go out to Gann's with you when we have the girl. We won't have her unless Lutz is stopped."

Slowly Vreeland nodded and extended his left hand. "I'll take the gun. You walk over to the jail. I'll see . . ."

"I don't give up the gun," Slattery said, his voice hard and tight for the first time. "They mean to kill that girl. She can identify Lutz and every member of that gang. I go along with you, Sheriff."

From the bedroom, Maria Perani called in Italian. Ugo said, "Maria, rest. Please. You must rest."

"Thomas would not do this to me," the woman answered. Her voice was weak, barely audible. "Sheriff, he would not harm a girl."

Slattery said to Vreeland, "I go with you to your office. I'll make Lutz tell the truth."

"Lutz isn't in the jail," said Vreeland. "He went to the station when I came over here."

"Then we'll go to the station together. I'll stay in front of you."

"I will come too," offered Ugo Perani. He stepped around the table to Slattery.

"You stay here," Vreeland told him. "That's why I came in, Ugo. Make sure the girl's mother and father don't try to go out. They could get caught in the middle." He moved toward Slattery and the rear door.

Ugo followed them, rubbing his hands together anxiously. The fear was gone from his face. He looked confident and hopeful. "For what they did to my wife," he said, "I should be with you."

Slattery said, "You should be with Maria, Ugo. She can't be left alone."

Ugo Perani simply nodded. He shut the door behind Slattery and the sheriff after they stepped out into the darkness of the yard.

In the doorway of the railroad station office, Paul Lutz pulled his visor lower over his forehead and adjusted his dust cuffs while he watched the engine chuffing into Rock Spring. The engineer had already started to apply the brakes. Heavy black smoke poured from the squat, barrel-like stack, blotting out the stars and horizon behind the tracks. The

148

entire station area was thick with the stinking smoke and cinder filth which had billowed from the train at his left while it had gotten up steam. Blended with the coal and soot, Lutz could smell frying onions and cabbage and fresh bread that was being prepared for supper in one of the town homes. Lutz smiled to himself. He hadn't been certain he could talk the sheriff into clearing the streets. Things had gone better than he'd planned. He noted that a few clouds had blown up to the north, but he wouldn't need them. Paxton and his gang were well enough hidden, despite the moonlight. After he left the money for them, Paxton knew his escape was up to him . . . Fireflies glowed on and off toward the corral and dragonflies swooped in twisted streaks of green. No matter how Lutz strained his eyes he couldn't see either a wagon or men on horses out there. They were there, he knew, or the second note wouldn't have been thrown into the general store . . .

Once more he reviewed everything he'd set into motion since yesterday. When he'd gone to Kansas to find Paxton, the gunman had agreed to the plan right away. It was so foolproof, from the taking of the girl, the Gann soddy for holding her, to his delivering of the money. The lamp was turned low in the office behind him, the desk's bottom drawer open for his share of the reward. Hughes had begged him to deliver it, Vreeland himself had heard that. The engine was a hundred yards away, brake chains clanging, steam hissing, groaning while it slowed. The conductor waved a lantern in a wide arc from the flat car where the stationery train clanged and chuffed, getting ready to move the instant the money reached the station.

Iron wheels screeched loudly against the tracks. Before the lone engine was fully stopped, a man in a black suit and a black bowler hat jumped down from the cab. He carried the black strapped satchel he held as though it was a great weight, walked directly to Lutz.

"We've got three guards hidden in the cab," the man said. "Can you use them?"

"Get them out of here!" Lutz answered fearfully. "The girl will be killed if we try anything."

"But the bank . . ."

"Move the engine! Both trains have to be out of here and the station clear before the money's delivered! Move it!"

The man backed away, ran toward the engine. Lutz stepped into the office, unbuckled the strap, opened the bag. The money was separated as the first note had directed. Small bills, divided into stacks of ten-thousand. Quickly Lutz picked out five stacks, dropped them into the open bottom drawer of the desk. His knee slid the desk drawer shut while he closed and strapped the black bag. A flick of the key in his hand and the desk was locked.

Outside the chuffing, clanging, groaning train engines had gotten up steam. The huge iron wheels were making their first slow turn in the din, would gradually pick up momentum.

Lutz straightened at the desk. He adjusted his visor, then his dust cuffs. He reached out to extinguish the lamp, but he changed his mind. Paxton could see him better against a background of light. Paxton could see better to shoot the girl when the time came.

Lutz waited, watched the backing engine slip out of his view through the window. The train was taking too much time, but it would move in a few moments.

Paul Lutz waited. His left hand brushed his coat, felt the small bulge of the derringer Vreeland had given him. Even that, he'd accomplished. In another minute he'd be outside and across the tracks. Nothing could go wrong . . .

"Trains are movin'," Joe Paxton said. "Get ready." He motioned to Baine, standing

151

beside Patricia Hughes. "Once Lutz crosses the tracks, let her go."

Patricia Hughes stared at Paxton. "I won't leave. If you're going to shoot me, do it now."

"Shoot you? Your family's payin' the money. It's all there or Lutz wouldn't be comin' out." Paxton gave a slight nod. "You walk when he's even with the corral."

Patricia Hughes did not answer, simply stared with the men at the railroad station. She knows, Paxton thought, but she's still hoping. He'd watched her this last half hour, had seen how she'd glanced around at the flat, too bright and clean under the moon. She hadn't given up her belief that Slattery would help her somehow. Paxton studied her. Her hair was mussed, dusty and streaked with dirt like her face and dress, from lying in the wagon so long under the canvas. She was so confident, her eyes still looking for help that wouldn't come.

Paxton gazed about the prairie, followed the girl's stare. He'd expected Fox would've ridden in before this. He knew Fox. He could've taken Slattery two or three miles away from Gann's and then killed him. Yet, because of the girl's confidence, Paxton wasn't as certain as he had been. He regretted he'd let Gann head out with his wagon. If trouble came, he'd be an extra gun. Paxton tried to

152

listen for sound along the prairie, but eh damned trains made too much racket.

"Keep watch around behind us," he told Allerby. "Listen for anything."

"Nobody's circlin' us," said Allerby. "Lutz wouldn't come out if the law's got men waitin'. That was our agreement, Joe. Lutz knows he better stick to it."

"Watch for Fox," Paxton said. "He'll be comin'."

Paxton reached behind him to his horse and pulled his Winchester from its boot. The lone engine had cleared the railroad platform. The train was passing the station, blocking the building from his view. Lutz would leave the office once the track was clear.

"Start walkin' soon as Lutz crosses the tracks," Paxton said to Patricia Hughes. "Just keep walkin'. Don't turn around and look back."

Slattery leaned forward in the long shadow of the building behind the railroad station and started his run. He'd waited here for a minute that had stretched like an hour for the train to take on motion. The stinking cinder smoke caught in his nostrils and he stifled a cough, took long-legged strides to the rear of the small building, then moved with his back flush along the side. The engine was even with the further end of the platform, the three passenger coaches stretched the length of the thick wooden planks, blocking the station from view of anyone out on the prairie. He didn't slow at the corner, turned in to the closed door, with Vreeland's toes at his bootheels. Slattery shoved the door open, stepped in where Paul Lutz stared, shocked and dumbfounded, at the desk.

Lutz's wide eyes dropped from Slattery to the Army .45 in Vreeland's hand. "What is this?" was all he could say before Slattery grabbed his arm and jerked him clear of the window. "You planned this whole kidnapping," Slattery said. He reached out, pulled the satchel from Lutz's hand.

"What! You're crazy, that's the ransom."

Lutz's hand had moved toward his right trouser pocket. Slattery swung from the hip. The uppercut whacked solidly against the neckline and chest and knocked the station agent slamming into the office's rear wall. Lutz folded, began to go down.

Slattery's fingers pulled, jerked at the buckle of the satchel strap.

Vreeland bent over Lutz's head. His revolver swung toward Slattery. "You didn't give him a chance. You've got no proof."

"Here's proof." Slattery opened the suitcase, held it low for the lawman to peer inside. "The note said ten piles of money. Only five are left. You look in this office, you'll find the other five."

"That still isn't enough . . ."

"It is for me." Slattery had thrown off his hat. "You'll have a gun on my back, Sheriff."

Dan Vreeland muttered to himself, then said, "What are you doin'?"

"The train's left." Slattery was slipping his coat free of his arms. "Stay low. Keep him down." He took the visor off Lutz's head, put it on his own, aware of the sharp finger of pain that flashed through his ear and neck at the touch against his wound.

"That money's my job," Vreeland said. "I should go out there."

"I'm as tall as Lutz. They'd spot you right away." He'd unhooked the dust cuffs, had one around his left wrist. He hooked the second in place. "Keep down. Don't try to help me."

Standing straight, Slattery buckled the suitcase strap while he stepped to the door. From the floor Dan Vreeland said, "You aren't wearin' a white shirt. They'll see."

Slattery heard him but he didn't slow. Opening the door, he stepped calmly onto the station platform.

Chapter Sixteen

The flat ahead was black and hazy beyond the glare of the bright station lamps. This must have all been part of Lutz's plan, Slattery thought, lighting the station so clearly Paxton could follow his every step. And Patricia Hughes would be just as clear in the sight of a rifle. Slattery slowed at the edge of the platform, carefully jumped down to the rails. He tilted his head slightly as his heels and soles touched the dirt. He kept his head lowered while he walked, as if he made certain nothing on the ground caused him to trip or fall in the moonlight.

The moon burned down like a noon sun, every ray of light on him making him stand out so plain he wondered why he hadn't been found out yet ... He raised the black satchel to the level of his stomach, hid the butt of the revolver that jutted from his belt. He could see the shape of the corral far ahead, but nothing near the dark fence of poles.

He kept walking.

One hundred yards from the corral, he first made out the shadows. Blots of darker night against the silver-white of the prairie, bunched up together. Horses and men, and a woman. None had left the group. They hadn't started Patricia Hughes in yet. He hefted the bag higher along his stomach. He'd hang it on the willow pole as the note had directed. After that, he didn't know what . . .

"I don't like it, Joe," said Allerby. The stubby gunman, his carbine in his hands, stood close to his mare in his hip-shot slouch. "He took too long comin' out of the station."

"It's Lutz," Paxton said irritably. He looked up at Baine who'd climbed into the saddle of his horse. "Give him a chance to get clear of the corral before you grab the bag. We'll cover you." He nudged Patricia Hughes. "Walk now. Not too fast."

The girl balked. "You're going to shoot . . ."

"Walk. We agreed you'd go back when we had the money. We're stickin' to that." He pushed her shoulder roughly. "You will get shot if you don't walk."

Patricia Hughes put her left foot out in front of her right. Then she took a second step. She wanted to scream. Up to this last minute, she'd held onto the belief, the hope, that somehow, somehow Slattery would come. Fox hadn't returned and something must have happened, and she'd believed in Slattery. The belief was gone, killed by the rough push Paxton had given her, and the reality of the two rifles behind her. They'd let her walk until Baine was safely away from the corral with the reward money . . .

Twenty steps behind her Paxton said loudly, "Ready, Baine? Allerby?"

Patricia closed her eyes, drove back the tears that wanted to come. She took one more step, another, watching the dark figure of Paul Lutz halt at the corral pole to hook on the suitcase. Lutz started to turn and retrace his steps. He was fifty feet from her. She wanted to scream out at him and accuse him, to tell everyone in the town over there what he'd done. But it was hopeless, useless. She was still too far away to be heard.

Horse's hoofs thumped behind her. At that moment Patricia Hughes began to cry.

Slattery heard the hoofbeats at the same instant as Patricia. The girl had been let go, he knew. She'd be even with the fence post where he'd left the satchel when the rider started back to the rest of Paxton's gang. They'd let her live only until the rider was clear of a shot from town. Only that long . . . Slattery slowed his step, kept both hands away from his sides, set one foot in front of the other like a man on a tightrope.

158

The hoofbeats drummed against the earth, became confused, and the rider spoke to the horse, growling at the animal while he came to an almost complete stop to grab the reward money.

Slattery took another step, another, knowing the girl's life depended on him. The horse kicked hardpack, whinnied painfully at the dig of a spur into its flank. Less than a minute now, Slattery knew. It wouldn't be Paxton on the horse. Paxton wouldn't shoot until his man was clear. Slattery had to chance it.

He glanced around across the bare open space. Patricia Hughes' small form was plainly silhouetted against prairie earth, the color of a whitish salt flat under the blazing moon. The rider had his mount heading away from the corral. It was Baine, the young one. He was half-turned in the saddle, looking directly at Slattery. Baine's face caught the brightness of the light, as clear and plain to Slattery as Slattery was to him.

Baine went for his gun. Slattery had his coming out, was turning to dash back toward Patricia as he fired.

The six-gun banged in his hand, loud as it was, the sound dulled, muffled by his voice bellowing to the girl.

"Run, Patricia! Run!" he yelled. "Run!"

Baine didn't get a shot off. He doubled over in the saddle, fought to hold on while his horse galloped wildly.

Slattery knew he should crouch, should zigzag to give a poorer target. He kept his body straight and tall, swung the revolver to the left and fired at the dark blots further along the flat, once, twice, his voice still bellowing, "Down! Fall down, Patricia! Roll toward the corral!"

Patricia doubled over, dropped to the ground. Directly behind her a rifle had slammed, then a second weapon. Slattery threw himself to the right, caught his footing, jerked to the left, heard the slugs hum like angry wasps past the spot he'd just vacated.

He had only three bullets left, wouldn't have time for a reload. Crouched low, he continued ahead, his weapon up, eyes on the dark form of Patricia Hughes frantically crawling for the upright corner post. The stretch of whitish ground between the girl and the corral looked a million miles across.

"Crawl! Crawl!" he yelled, triggering off a fourth precious bullet at the area where he'd seen the barrel flashes.

Chapter Seventeen

Allerby hardly understood what had happened, it had happened so fast. He'd had his rifle up and aimed, his stare on Baine heading back from the corral. The thought of fifty-thousand to split three ways controlled his thoughts, when all hell had broken loose. Baine had yelled something, blurting out about, "No white shirt!" and Lutz had shot him.

The voice Allerby heard yelling wasn't Lutz's but Slattery's and Paxton had fired and hollered for him to shoot.

Slattery's bullets had zinged past, barely missing the horses. "Spread out! Spread out!" Paxton screamed. "Split the target."

Now Paxton watched the fourth spark of flame spit from Slattery's gun. He triggered off one bullet to keep Slattery down, the man was so low along the ground, weaving so he couldn't be hit. Two more bullets Slattery had at the most ... Paxton pumped two more slugs at the hazy, zigzagging shadow. Baine was twenty feet away, hugging the horse's neck. The girl completely forgotten, Paxton ran to stop Baine's mount.

"Scatter your fire," he shouted to Allerby. "Keep him down! Back to the horses!"

Allerby opened up, got off one, two, three bullets Paxton kept track of. Paxton ran alongside Baine's horse, grabbed at the bridle to slow the animal. Then he saw that both of Baine's arms circled the horse's neck. Baine's face pressed into the mane.

"The money!" Paxton said. "Where's the money!"

Baine blubbered incoherently.

Paxton had the horse stopped. "Where's the money!"

"D . . . dropped . . . drop . . ." Baine began to slip from the saddle.

"Dropped!" Paxton whirled away from the horse, stared at the corral. Allerby's rifle pounded in his ear, the noise lost to him while his eyes sought for and found the money satchel, a black spot on the ground, a hundred feet this side of the corral.

Paxton headed for his stallion. "Keep him down," he screamed at Allerby. "I'll get the money."

"Wha . . ." Allerby looked around momentarily, saw Baine's horse's saddle was empty. Baine had fallen to the ground.

"He's hit. Help him," Allerby began.

"Keep Slattery down! I'll get the money!" Paxton leaped into the saddle, held his carbine as an Indian would a lance. "Kill Slattery!" He kicked his spurs, brought the carbine around to shoot as the stallion charged ahead.

Allerby fired once. Slattery's gun spit flame and Paxton heard Allerby's loud grunt when the lead bullet struck. One bullet left, Paxton thought, spurring the stallion again. One bullet between himself and Slattery and the money and the girl he'd kill before he left. He jerked at the reins, wheeled the horse, squeezed the trigger and pumped his weapon for another shot while he bore down on Slattery.

Slattery backed a step, then another, realizing what Paxton meant to do. Intent on drawing the rider as far as he could from the corral, he couldn't see the man's face because of the way he kept his head behind the horse's neck.

From behind him came confused violent sounds of motion as loud as the horse's clomping. A voice shouted to him. The words were lost as he chanced a side-stepping leap to the right to get a full view of the rider. It was Paxton. The weapon in the gunman's hands flashed a third shot while Slattery aimed the Colt.

The side-step threw him clear of the bullet. His own struck along Paxton's right side, he knew from the sudden jerk of the mounted

163

man's body. But Paxton wasn't through.

The stallion kept coming, Paxton crouched a bit, his carbine in both hands. Slattery ran backwards. The Colt drum snapped open in his hand, the fingers of his left shoving the first of the cartridges he'd drawn from his pocket into the chamber.

The yell came then, so loud Paxton heard. A rifle banged in the darkness behind Slattery.

The bullet didn't hit Paxton, yet it was enough to draw his attention. He fired past Slattery's head, pumped his weapon smooth and fast as he again turned it on Slattery.

Slattery's right hand had flicked the drum shut. He shot Paxton square in the chest. Paxton dropped his carbine, tumbled from the saddle like a heavy felled log before the stallion galloped past Slattery.

Slattery didn't pause. He glanced behind him at the one who'd saved him, saw the man was down, prostrate on the ground.

Ugo Perani waved at Slattery from where he lay. "Go. Go, Thomas. The little girl!" Slattery was already headed away from him.

Slattery had the revolver broken, slowed enough to insert two more cartridges. He moved forward quickly, not certain the other two gunmen could continue the fight, ready to finish it if they waited . . .

Allerby lay on his side, his stubby body motionless, a Henry carbine still gripped in his right hand. Slattery's booted toe hooked along the stock and threw the weapon away from the curled fingers. The body rolled onto its back, showed an ugly bloody gash where the collarbone met at the throat.

Slattery held the Colt downward, walked quickly toward Baine. The gunman groaned, low and weak, did not look up as the footsteps halted. He was doubled over holding both knees hard against his groin and belly, his groans part of every difficult breath of air he gagged into his lungs. His holster was empty. No rifle or six-gun was on the ground close to him.

Slattery crouched above him, decided the best thing to do was leave him until he could be carefully moved. A voice hailed words that weren't clear to him from the direction of town. Straightening he dropped the three cartridges he held in his left hand into his trouser pocket. He jammed the Colt under his belt buckle, aware of the people who crowded onto the flat now, conscious of the burning sensation along the right side of his head and ear.

Blood wet his fingers when he touched the hairline. The wound had reopened while he'd moved fast to shift his position; it smarted and stung more than it had when Fox's bullet had grazed him. The figures in the moonlight were only dark gray blurs some of them running to where Ugo Perani lay, but most following like a tight-packed herd behind Dan Vreeland and Paul Lutz.

The voice which had hailed him came through the silence, stunning to his ears after all the pounding gunblasts. Patricia Hughes' call sounded as thin and thrilling as a distant bugle.

Slattery walked back to meet the lawman. The girl hurried from the far side of the corral with her long skirt raised above her ankles. He felt light-headed and heavy-footed. He had expected to be cut down by the three, and he was living. He'd been a part of this whole thing when it had started, and he'd hoped only to give the girl time to get away. The fight had all happened so fast, he needed time himself to calm the hot and cold fingers of nerves that tightened and loosened up and down his chest and stomach.

Lutz came ahead in long strides. He threw a glance at Patricia Hughes. She was still twenty feet from him and the sheriff when they met Slattery.

"Baine's the only one left," Slattery told Vreeland. "He'll have to be moved easy."

"This one'll help," the lawman snapped.

166

He pointed to the bodies in the moonlight. Jack Kennedy, a step behind his boss, grabbed Lutz's shoulder. "He'll carry one end, Jack," added Vreeland. "He tries anything, make it four out here. For what he did, hit him where it'll be slow for him."

"I will, Dan. Don't worry."

"That man was one of them," Patricia Hughes said coming in close to them. She halted so she stared into Lutz's frightened face. Lutz wouldn't look at her. "I heard their talk while they held me. He thought up the entire plan. Every last idea was his."

"I found fifty-thousand in the station desk," Vreeland said. He watched Lutz walk off with his deputy. He gazed at the townspeople who crowded toward the bodies, and the black satchel which held the ransom money.

"Mr. Osgood," he called to a white-haired old man. "Pick up that bag and take it to the jail, will you?" He didn't wait for the man's answer, went on to Patricia Hughes, "Your parents are waitin'. I'll take you back."

The girl nodded. She stared at Slattery. "I waited, hoping and believing. At the end I'd given up. I had."

Slattery grinned. "I had myself." She edged closer, her face inches from his, looking at him. Her hair was mussed, streamed over her forehead and along the right side of her face and neck. Her dress was torn across the shoulder, was peppered and streaked with dirt and dust. Her eyes were wet and shining. She was truly beautiful, he thought, more so now, and freer somehow. "I had my doubts, Pat."

She smiled. Vreeland touched her arm. "It's hard only on your mother and father now, girl. They agreed to wait." He turned with the young woman, shot a glance at Slattery. "You want to come with us after Gann? I don't figure they'll be anything to take."

"No, Sheriff." Slattery left them and headed toward the small crowd that helped Ugo Perani get to his feet.

The fat hotelman was plainly visible in the center of four men who all but fought to carry him. Two were making a chair by crossing their arms and gripping wrists. Ugo's bald head reflected the soft light, turned in Slattery's direction to speak to him.

"How are you, Ugo?" said Slattery.

"Fine. I am fine, Thomas. The bullet grazed only the side of my leg." He beamed a wide grin. "We did well, Thomas."

"You took such a chance, Ugo."

The grin vanished and the Italian's voice calmed. "For what they did to my Maria. And the terrible fear of the kidnapping. It was for that, and you."

Slattery touched the round shoulder, moved along beside the men. "Thank you, Ugo. Thank you." The jumbled nerves had calmed some, then quieted even more while he walked from the flat and across the emptiness of the railroad tracks into Rock Spring, talking easily with Ugo Perani.

Boulder Street was empty at the corner. The crowd that had formed thronged at the jail doorway and bulged out in a solid tight-packed line across the wide roadway to the Sorento House porch. William Hughes and his wife saw Slattery. Together they left the group and walked to meet him. Hughes' small thin face showed his happiness, yet his voice was a blend of anxiety and seriousness.

"We want to thank you, Mr. Slattery," he said. "For what you've done. For every-thing."

Mrs. Hughes looked greyish and worn out, the strain lines cut deep into her forehead and around her mouth. "Both of us, Mr. Slattery." Her eyes went to Ugo Perani. The men who carried him were almost to his hotel now. "And Mr. Perani." Her stare returned to Slattery. "We were so wrong."

"I don't know how to . . ." her husband began. Patricia Hughes had moved in beside her father. She touched his arm softly, looked as gently at her mother. "Tom should see about his head," she said. "You can talk all you want later. You'll have time on the train tomorrow."

Slattery looked from Patricia to Sheriff Vreeland. The lawman's tiny black eyes studied the girl, then met Slattery's. Beyond Vreeland men and horses had started to gather, every man wearing a coat against the night chill, each of them armed. Rube Whaleen, the bartender from the Drovers, sprawled across his saddle horn, his eyes on Slattery and the woman. The same curious expression was on his face as on Vreeland's.

"Well, I won't be going toward Fort Worth," Slattery said. "I'll get patched up and cut 'cross country to San Saba."

"But you'll need rest," Mrs. Hughes offered. "You poor man . . ."

"He'll get rest," Vreeland told her. "I'll give him a call when we get back in. I'll have Lutz wire for a train early tomorrow for you folks."

Patricia Hughes' gaze flicked from Vreeland to Slattery.

"Well, I'll get patched up," said Slattery. He touched the small trickle of blood above his ear, visibly winced at the smarting. Men and women opened a path to allow him to head for the hotel. Those at the rear and the sides broke off, walked in small groups toward the residential section.

Mrs. Hughes' features brightened, turned to her husband. "A stagecoach," she said. "The stagecoach line goes through San Saba."

Her husband didn't have time to answer, for their daughter said, "I'd thought of that. One can leave in the morning."

"Then we'll take it, dear," her mother began.

Patricia Hughes shook her head. "You and father will be on the train, Mother." Mrs. Hughes opened her lips to speak, but Patricia was emphatic.

"You can rest and wait in Fort Worth." She stared past the heads of the few people who'd remained to talk among themselves along the roadway. Slattery had crossed the hotel porch. His tall, wide-shouldered form filled the doorway, was gone into the lobby. "I'll be perfectly all right."

She'd go to San Saba, that was definite. Yet, after the way Slattery had left, the only accomplishment she felt sure of was that finally she actually was making her own decisions and doing what she wanted, alone.

m